I0565653

STANDING IN THE GAP

A Gullah Novel

Sherman E. Pyatt

EVENING POST
BOOKS

Published by
Evening Post Books
Charleston, South Carolina

Copyright © 2024 Sherman E. Pyatt
All rights reserved.
First edition

Author: Sherman E. Pyatt
Editor: John M. Burbage
Designer: Gill Guerry

No part of this book may be reproduced or transmitted in any form or by any means, electronic or mechanical, including photocopying, recording or by information storage and retrieval system – except by a reviewer who may quote brief passages in a review to be printed in a magazine, newspaper, or on the web – without permission in writing from the publisher. For information, please contact the publisher.

First printing 2024

Printed in the United States of America

A CIP catalog record for this book has been applied for from the Library of Congress.

ISBN: 978-1-929647-98-9

– Dedicated to –
Shomari and Sean, my sons; and Marilyn, my wife,
for their unending support and encouragement.
You have been with me from the beginning. And
to all of those sea islanders who lived and thrived in
those remote areas for centuries.

– In Memory of –
Corey B. Dennis Sr. (nephew),
Ronald C. Williams (brother) and
Parkie Pyatt (daughter-in-law)
who are always in my thoughts.

– Acknowledgments –
I am indebted to Evening Post Books for
accepting my manuscript and believing that this
was a work worthy of publishing. I am especially
indebted to my editor, John M. Burbage, for
his guidance and professionalism — thank
you for your literary expertise. Although many
people encouraged and assisted me, I take full
responsibility for any omissions or errors that may
appear in this work.

 PREFACE

This novel, much of it written in Gullah, is about African American family life and culture from 1915 to 1917 along the South Carolina coast — specifically Wadmalaw Island — and in the nearby port city of Charleston.

Most islanders, descendants of enslaved Central and West Africans, stayed close to home until bridges were built in 1926. These largely isolated African Americans became known as Sea Islanders. Their ancestors began arriving in Charleston in the 1700s and were sold to owners of coastal South Carolina indigo, rice and sea cotton plantations, where they lived, worked and died one generation to the next for more than three centuries.

They developed a culture of blended African and American customs that included Gullah — a Creole dialect and native-inspired arts, crafts, cuisine, and religion. The Gullah-influenced Sea Islands span as far north as Wilmington, NC, to as far south as St. Augustine, FL — a stretch known as the Gullah Geechee Corridor.

Although freedom came to all African Americans after the Civil War, numerous Gullah and Geechee families remained isolated on bridgeless Atlantic islands where they continued to work the land, the rivers and the sea. It wasn't until the early 1900s that a major demographic change began with the Great Migration from the rural, racially repressive South to large cities in the North, Midwest and California — wherever railroad tracks took them in search of relatives and better-paying jobs. By 1970 an estimated six million black, Southern Americans had moved to Philadelphia, New York, Chicago, Detroit and Los Angeles.

This story is about the Logan/Rouse line of Wadmalaw Island, a typical Gullah family except for pre-teen Jacob Daniel Rouse, who like his late Grandfather Big Leon Logan possessed a pronounced spiritual connection. The novel begins on a warm summer afternoon with the arrival of a midwife at Jacob's grandmother's house, where the boy's aunt is about to deliver her first child. It's a novel like no other, abundant in African American tradition and expressed largely in a Gullah dialect, which most readers will find enlightening as well as enjoyable.

To understand what the characters are saying, readers should pay attention to the context of sentences and the sound of the words, not the spellings. A Gullah glossary is included in the book as needed. Gullah is a Creole language combining West African and English words. Consider reading the book aloud to yourself or with friends and family, in church groups, book clubs, classrooms and the like. Readers should consider expressing each sentence in context before trying to commit specific word and phrase meanings to memory. It gets easier and more engaging as you continue.

The characters herein are fictitious, but the places are real. My grandmother was born in 1903 on Wadmalaw Island, and I spent several summers on the island with my cousins experiencing a different environment from the city of Charleston where I grew up twenty miles away.

Like the main character in this book, I was born "with the veil," the spiritual meaning of which will be explained forthwith through the life of young Jacob Rouse. I have researched Gullah Geechee culture extensively and have written several books and articles on the history and traditions of African Americans of the South Carolina Lowcountry and coastal Georgia. There is a wealth of wisdom available via these people, and I am happy to share some of it with you.

Sherman E. Pyatt
Charleston, South Carolina

CHAPTER 1

Jacob Rouse, 11, sits on the top step of the front porch, hands over his ears to muffle screams from Aunt Charlotte's bedroom. She has been screeching and crying for hours, and it rattles through his head like echoes in a cave.

"Jacob! Jacob! Weh yah at?" his grandmother, Mary Logan, yells from inside the two-room, heart-pine house on Wadmalaw Island, about halfway down the coast of South Carolina near Charleston.

"Yes ma'am," Jacob says as he heads up the porch to the front door. His grandmother stands at the cast-iron kitchen sink squeezing her daughter Charlotte's sweat from a washcloth, which Mary rinses in a bucket of water Jacob has drawn from the handpump outside at the end of the porch near the kitchen window.

"Go find Miss Ella Mae. De tide up in de creek, so her ent far down de road now. Baby comin'…"

"Yes ma'am!" Jacob says, turns, takes two long strides across the porch, jumps all three steps into the yard and sidesteps a puddle of early morning rain. He sprints down the dirt lane that winds through palmetto, pine, oak and other hardwood trees until he reaches a washout over which is a wide, wooden plank for crossing. He steps carefully onto the board and shuffles to the other side. He mops his brow with a shirt sleeve, squints through the morning mist and sees a woman with a large satchel in one hand and a crooked walking stick in the other.

"Mornin', Miss Ella Mae!" Jacob shouts as he runs to her.

"Who dat?"

"Dis me, Jacob Rouse. Sho' glad to see yah. Baby comin' soon …"

The midwife places her worn, leather satchel on the ground, hugs Jacob and searches his eyes, wide open with anxiety. He wraps his arms around her narrow waist and rests his head on her chest.

"Yah almos' tall as dat oleander in yah' grandma's yard, boy. Huh ol' yuh is now?"

"I's eleben, Miss Ella Mae.

"Eleben? Dat one year mo' than ten, init? … Is you marri'd yet?"

He looks up at her with half a smile. *"No ma'am, I too lil' fuh dat."*

She rubs the top of his head. *"Come on, Jacob. Us got work to do."*

"Wan' me tote yah satchel?"

She smiles. *"Yah ent too tired from all dat runnin'? Dat ting heaby."*

"No ma'am, ent too heaby."

He grabs the bag — dark brown leather top to bottom, stuffed with herbs, a bottle of witch hazel, a jar of rubbing alcohol, clean towels, a razor-sharp knife and medicine vials. The midwife, with a crooked hickory stick in hand, and the boy each ease across the plank and around various puddles, and they say nothing until they reach the oleander tree at Mary Logan's house. Ella Mae, 55, is the only midwife for a string of six coastal islands below Charleston to the south branch of the Edisto River. She is slim, only five-feet-three inches tall. She learned about birthing from her grandmother, who delivered at least forty babies before she died fourteen years ago. Ella Mae has brought twelve more, including Jacob Rouse, into the world since then.

"Jacob, huh Charlotte do'n?" the midwife asks as they reach the porch.

"Her be in de bed cryin' all morn'n'. Nana say yah comin', buh ent do no good. Her ent stop crying."

"Sweet Charlotte go' drop dat baby t'day," Ella Mae says as she climbs the steps. She leans her stick on the wall by the door and takes the satchel from Jacob. His grandmother greets them at the door.

"Mornin', Sistuh Mary. Huh hunnuh fuh duh?" the midwife asks.

"Mornin', Miss Ella Mae. I doin' fine. Buh I all shook up wid dis gal."

Mary is the widow of Leon Logan Sr., nicknamed Big Leon, who died in a hunting accident not long after Jacob was born. Mary is younger than Ella Mae by five years. The Logan family has lived on Wadmalaw since long before the Civil War, which the locals still describe as "When Gun Shoot," as if the fighting began just the other day. The islanders could hear the cannon sixty miles down the coast when a fleet of U.S. Navy vessels opened fire on Confederate forts on Hilton Head Island and Bay Point strategically placed at the mouth of Port Royal Sound. Soon afterward, Union troops invaded lower South Carolina through the sound and Beaufort. "Gun Shoot" was the sound of freedom, Big Leon used to say.

Mary has four children: Jacob's mother, Anna Logan Rouse, a widower and seamstress who lives and works in Charleston; Leon Logan Jr., a fisherman, also in Charleston; Peter Logan, a carpenter who lives with his wife on Edisto Island; and Charlotte Logan Pringle, who is in labor at this moment in Mary's bedroom.

Mary leads the midwife into the bedroom and Ella Mae puts her satchel on the floor, which is sprinkled with moss and green pine needles, the scent of which helps keep gnats, flies and other bugs at bay. It's June, hot and humid inside and out of the house despite the morning shower. Ella Mae places her palm on Charlotte's forehead.

"Hush now, Charlotte. Ready to hab yah baby?"

 # CHAPTER 2

Charlotte, who turned nineteen last month, is the youngest of Mary's children. She is married to Benjamin Pringle, a dockworker in Charleston about thirty miles away as the crow flies, triple that by boat. Charlotte is dark and thin with coarse, medium-length, curly hair typical of the Wadmalaw Logans, whose complexions range from deep black to light brown. Her skin is rich in color, like sea island soil, which at one time grew the most valuable long-staple cotton in the world.

"Us go hab dis baby t'day," the midwife again vows softly, wiping Charlotte's forehead with a damp cloth. *"Sistuh Mary, pull dem curtain back frum de window an' open 'em wide. Need mo' air. Bring clean sheet an' two towel, an' put big pot ob water on de stobe."*

Mary opens the curtains and the window then hustles past Jacob, who is sitting in the main room while leaning left, then right trying to see what's happening in the bedroom. His grandmother pours water in a large iron pot, slips three short pieces of dried oak onto the coals inside the kitchen stove, hurries past Jacob back into the bedroom and shuts the door. Charlotte's screeching and crying resumes as Jacob closes his eyes and waits — he doesn't know how long until — BANG! The bedroom door slams open against the bedroom wall and Mary hollers:

"Jacob, go to de woodpile ... Grab dat hand axe fuh me. Hurry!"

Jacob runs out, leaps over all three porch steps, dodges the puddle, passes the outhouse to the woodpile. He grabs the axe and returns to the porch, where his grandmother awaits him. She takes the axe back into the bedroom and closes the door. Jacob stands on the porch and listens as Charlotte's screams give way to whimpers. He sits in his grandmother's wide, oak porch rocker, which squeaks with each pivot. He tries to clear his head by focusing on two chicken hens — one black, the other white — scratching in the dirt by the porch and fussing like they always do. He wonders why they can't get along with each other. He's drenched in sweat and humidity of the late-morning sun, which filters through long beards of gray moss drooping from muscular limbs of a large oak tree beside the house. A gentle Atlantic breeze reaches Jacob's bare legs. He closes his eyes; his mind drifts to a shallow bend in Rouse's Creek where he splashes with his cousin Emma and two other children. He relaxes until the bedroom door bangs open again …

"Tank yah Jedus! Tank yah Lawd!" Mary shouts. *"Yah gimme a gran'dau'tuh today. Tank yah Jedus!"*

Jacob jumps up from the rocker. *"Baby come?"*

"Oh yeah," Mary says, standing in the front room and grinning.

"Nana, why yah cryin' and laughing at the same time?" Jacob asks as he looks into her eyes.

"Chil', dis tear a joy!"

"Nana, can I see de baby now?"

"Be a lil' while. Miss Ella Mae ent through yet."

The midwife calls for Mary, who returns to the bedroom, and Jacob hears the baby crying. About a half-hour later, his grandmother opens the bedroom door. *"Jacob, come see yah new cuz'n."*

He follows her into the bedroom and eyes Charlotte sitting upright in the bed with clean sheets and pillows behind her head and back. She holds the baby to her breast while the midwife carries an armful of used towels and bed sheets outside and places them in a washtub beside the pump.

"Jacob," Charlotte whispers, *"come close."*

"Can I touch her?" he asks.

Before Charlotte could answer, Mary says, *"Only touch she foot fuh now."*

Jacob feels the baby's feet, then each toe, and smiles. The midwife returns and taps Jacob on the shoulder.

"Teke dis broom an' sweep out all dat moss an' straw, an' tote dat bucket wuh hab dat cloth obuh 'um to de porch," she says.

"Yes ma'am."

Jacob sweeps the floor around the bed and peeks at the baby while Mary and the midwife sit at the table near the kitchen.

"Stay for a while," Mary says to the midwife. *"Tide ent high yet."*

CHAPTER 3

After Mary and the midwife talk about nothing in particular for a while, Mary goes to the stove and adds wood for another pot of hot water. *"I fixin' swimp perlo, cornbread an' grit tea fuh yah, Ella Mae,"* she says. Mary has made this popular shrimp-and-rice dish also known as "pilaf," but the tea, which is steeped in corn grits, is a rarity.

Meanwhile, Jacob sweeps the moss and pine straw out onto the porch and into the yard. He returns to the bedroom, kneels down, reaches under the bed and pulls out the axe, which is wiped clean already. He carries it out past the cloth-covered bucket on the porch and back to the woodpile.

"Wuh yah want me to do wid dat bucket on the po'ch?" Jacob asks his grandmother after he gets back to the house.

"Leab 'em fuh now."

"Wuh in dat bucket, and why de towel on 'um?"

Mary pauses … *"I tell yah later."*

Jacob sits in the porch rocker and listens to the ladies talking inside.

"Dat baby bootiful," the midwife says, *"weigh at leas' six pound."*

Mary grins. *"I go meke dat tea now. Wan' some? I boil up de grits early dis mornin'…"* She lifts a large cast-iron frying pan full of cooled, finely ground corn seasoned and boiled, each bit swollen with salted water.

"I ent hab grit tea in Lawd only kno' when," Ella Mae says.

Mary flips the hardened grits from the pan onto her chopping board and cuts them into four squares. She puts a spoonful of solidified bacon fat into the pan and places it on the hot stove top. Once heated, but not too much, she spoons each little cake into the pan. When a cake sizzles brown on one side, she flips it over and so forth until all are sizzled brown on the other. She pours two cups of hot water over the cakes and drains the drippings into two coffee mugs, one of which she hands to the midwife. Mary adds a teaspoon of local honey to each cup.

Ella Mae takes a sip. *"Oh, Miss Mary, das good!"*

After listening for a while, Jacob returns to the bedroom, peeks at the baby and studies old newspaper pages pasted on the walls for insulation. He's a good student, and can read most of the words on the newsprint about things and places he's never seen. He walks softly across the floor, careful not to wake up Charlotte and the baby. A wide pinewood-floorboard squeaks as he slips out the door, which he shuts gently behind him.

"Don' close 'um tight," his grandmother says.

"Yes ma'am," he says then sits at the table with the ladies.

"Jacob, yah born 'bout dis time of year, ent yah?" Ella Mae asks.

Mary doesn't give him a chance to answer, *"Ella Mae, huh long yuh teke to bring Jacob into de worl'?"*

The midwife smiles. *"Dat boy fight me frum dayclean an' through de night … Lawd hab mussy … Lemme tink some mo' on dat … Uh-huh, uh-huh, I 'membuh now. Jacob wuh born early de next day … and wid de veil over 'e head."*

Mary stands up, places her hands on her hips. *"Folk say dem dat hab de veil can read dream an' see spirrut an' ting like dat."*

"Oh yeah," the midwife says and looks at Jacob. *"Dat veil cover yah head aftuh yah leebe yuh momma womb.' Dat special. Yah de only one like dat I kno'. Jacob, do yah dream a lot?*

Jacob smiles. Indeed, he does dream a lot, and a recurring one lately is about a man standing in the front door of Mary's house and staring in at him … But before he answers, his grandmother says:

"Sistuh, I glad yah ax dat. I tink Jacob hab sump'n to do wid Charlotte baby comin' dis day … Jacob say he been dreamin' 'bout cleanin' fush and de fush scale get on 'e arm. De ol' folk say when someone born wid de veil dream 'bout fush, somebody in de fambly go' hab a baby … And dat ent all. Jacob fush hab scale on him — dat mean baby go' be a girl.

"Hush yuh mout'!" Ella Mae whispers.

"Dat right. Dey say when someone born wid de veil dream 'bout fush widout no scale, baby go' be a boy. Well … last year Jacob say 'e dream 'bout a sha'ak, wuh got mout full a teete but ent got no scale … Ella Mae, ent yah delibuh Cuz'n Ruby baby in Rockville las' April?"

"Dat right, Sistuh," the midwife responds.

"Wuh her hab?

"A boy!" Ella Mae says.

Jacob reaches down and pretends to tie his brogan shoe because he doesn't want the ladies to see him grinning. Ella Mae is about to say something else when Mary looks over at her grandson:

"Jacob, go get a bucket ob water fuh me."

"Yes ma'am," he says, grabs an empty bucket by the sink and goes out to the porch pump. He fills the bucket then moves under the kitchen window, which is open, and listens some more:

"Jacob got dat birthmark on 'e back," Mary says.

"Dat de mark de ol' folk talk 'bout?" the midwife asks.

"Yes ma'am, Sistuh, dat de mark … 'e got the mark and de veil.

Jacob's birthmark is circular, about the size of a quarter, and in the center of the circle is a cross. Older islanders say life never ends for the bearer, who also has healing powers. They claim that such a person has been coming and going to Wadmalaw for almost four hundred years.

Jacob returns with the bucket full of water. The midwife steps out on the porch and points to the other bucket — the one with the cloth covering the top that she filled after the baby was born:

"Jacob, I go tell yah wuh to do wid wuh en dat bucket." She slides it with her foot closer to Jacob and removes the cloth. *"In dis bucket is wuh keep dat baby alibe inside yah Aunt Charlotte."*

Jacob looks down, sees blood and what looks like the skinned eel his Uncle Leon had caught in the creek and cleaned in the yard the last time he was on the island.

"Jacob, dat oleander tree out dey be plant by yuh grandmomma de day yuh born. Teke dat bucket out and bury wuh inside next to 'um," the midwife says. *"Plant 'um deep and not too close cause us go gro' anudduh tree out dere fuh yah new cousin.*

"Yes ma'am," he says, grabs the bucket and heads out front.

Mary walks to the door and asks the midwife: *"Yah 'membuh when us at de church las' year an' I tell you Jacob dream 'bout a funeral?"*

"Uh-huh."

"Well, de ol' folk say when somebody wid de veil dream 'bout a funeral, go' be a wedd'n', an' when 'e dream 'bout a wedd'n', go' be a funeral."

"Uh-huh," Ella Mae says.

"Well, Sistuh, dis no lie, ent long aftuh dat, Benjamin come to de house an' ax to marry Charlotte."

"Fuh true?" Ella Mae asks.

"As Gawd my widnuss standin' in front ob yah!"

Ella Mae eyes Jacob walking around the oleander tree and says:

"Yah sho' bout dat?"

"Yes ma'am. Jacob dream a lot 'bout all kind a ting. Dat boy got Charlotte so scay'd talkin' 'bout a dream, she almos' drop dat baby out in de ya'd!

"Wuh happ'n?"

"Well, I out dere pullin' green bean early in de mo'nin' while Jacob an' Charlotte in de house. I look up an' hey come Charlotte walkin' fas', pullin' Jacob by 'e hand. So, I ax, 'Wuh wrong?' Charlotte say Jacob see a man standin' in de door, buh dey ent no man standin' in the door. So I ax Jacob why him say dat? Jacob look at me, an' say a man be standin' in the door, an' I kno' dat boy ent lying."

"Huh yuh kno' dat?" the midwife asks.

"Jacob ent blink 'e eye, dat why, an' 'e say, 'Nana, I see 'um, I see 'um!' Den 'e sta't cryin' 'cause I ent b'leeb him at fust."

"Wuh yah do aftuh dat?"

"I tell Jacob to go back to de house, and I remind Charlotte dat when Jacob bo'n, 'e special, accordin' to de old folk, dat 'e hab de veil on 'e head, an' dat mark on 'e shoulder, an' he see spirrut, an' talk to 'em too … Dat when Charlotte say, 'Momma, Jacob my nephew, an' I lub dat boy, but him spooky!' So I tell Charlotte, 'Gal, spirrut ent go hurt yah!' And Charlotte say, 'Den us ent talk 'bout dat no mo'. OK?"

Ella Mae says nothing.

"Sistuh," Mary continues, *"when Jacob be eight, us on de porch an' he say dem tree out dere talk to him. I jump up out de chair an' listen, but I ent hey nutt'n'."*

"Yah tink Jacob hea' dem tree talkin'?" Ella Mae asks.

"Yes ma'am."

"So dat why Charlotte skay'd?"

Mary nods affirmatively, and the ladies laugh nervously. Then Mary continues with her story:

"When I got back, I rub de sweat off Jacob face and say I ent angry wid him. I tell 'um dat if 'e eber see that man again, don' say nuttin' to Charlotte … Dat boy look up wid a puzzle look an' ax me, 'Huccome Charlotte ent see de man standin' in the door?' I tell 'um 'e special, wid a gif' mos' people ent got. I ax 'um not to say nuttin' to Charlotte 'bout dat no mo'. Jacob look at me wid 'e big, wide eye and say, 'Alright Nana'."

Ella Mae leans forward and whispers:

"Who de man standin' in de door?"

"I tink 'e Big Leon, Gawd bless 'e soul, come back to see 'e grandson."

"Huh you tink dat, Mary?"

"I ax Jacob to 'scribe de man, an' Jacob 'scribe 'e granddaddy 'xactly — including de hat 'e hab on when 'e out in de boat … Big Leon pass not long aftuh Jacob born. I ent know huh dat boy 'membuh wuh Big Leon look like."

Moments later Jacob returns to the room.

"'Scuse me Nana."

"Uh huh," she says.

"Um. Um. If dat oleander tree die, dat mean I go die too?"

Mary and Ella Mae look at each other, then Mary reaches over to Jacob and pulls him close:

"No son, yah spirrut and muh spirrut and Miss Ella Mae spirrut ent nebuh go be dead, eben aftuh us gone frum hea'. Unduhstan' wuh I sayin'?"

"I tink so."

 # CHAPTER 4

The tide is almost high as Ella Mae packs her satchel. *"Mary, huh long you bin in dis house?"*

"Well, lemme see … Big Leon build'um dis place in 18 and 87 or 88, sump'n' like dat."

"Hurricane ebuh hit yah?"

"Oh, no Sistuh, tank Gawd."

Ella Mae nods. *"De Lawd good to yah fuh sho'. Wuh 'xactly happ'n to Big Leon?"*

"Well … 'e go huntin' at Moss Creek, an hab accident," Mary said, shaking her head, rubbing her hands.

"Sistuh Mary, you ent hafuh talk 'bout dis if yuh ent wanna."

Mary says, *"I talk 'bout Big Leon 'cause I nebuh wanna fuhgit dat man."*

"OK Sistuh … I listnin'."

Mary sits back in her chair. *"Lemme see … ent bin long aftuh Jacob born when Big Leon go out 'bout sunrise by de rice pon' and sit fuh dem duck to come. He hear 'em, den 'e see 'em circle round and sta't to land, an' he jump up to shoot … buh 'e drop dat gun, an' BANG … 'e shot hisself en 'e head and fall back on de ground."*

Moss Creek Plantation is south of Wadmalaw on Edisto Island. The owner is Jacob Fleming, who grew up on an estate that belonged to his father, James

Fleming, a white man and widower. Jacob Fleming's mother was an African-American house servant named Sally. They never married. After he passed away, his son bought the Moss Creek property with money his father left him.

"*Jacob Fleming a good man,*" Mary continues. "*Muh Jacob be name aftuh him. Muh oldest daughter, Anna, be Jacob momma. Anna an' she husband Daniel Rouse wuh married only three mont' when he drown in Rouse Creek. So when de baby come, Big Leon ax Anna to name her son Jacob Daniel Rouse fuh boff she late husband an' Mr. Fleming.*"

"*It wasn't long aftuh dat when Big Leon pass. I felt sump'n wrong de mornin' 'e lef' de house. At 'bout midday Cuz'n Elijah come say Big Leon hurt bad, dat 'e drop 'e gun an' all. Elijah teke me en 'e boat to Mr. Fleming house on Edisto.*"

Mary described the house as having tall ceilings, two stories, shiny heart-pine floors and two winding staircases. She said Mr. Fleming greeted her at the top of the steps, and they walked together into the bedroom where Big Leon was being treated by Dr. Johnson, of Charleston, who was on the island making his quarterly rounds. Dr. Johnson was born and raised in Charleston and worked at what folks called the "Colored Hospital."

"*Big Leon in de bed wid 'e head 'rap up. Dr. Johnson ax me to sit down next to 'um, an' 'e say: 'Miss Mary, yuh husband ent' go' meke it ... nuttin' mo' I can do. Stay wid him now ... I be back soon.' ... Well, Leon look bad layin' de bed. Dat when 'e open one eye and say, 'Mary, das you?' I grab 'e hand an' squeeze 'um. 'Yeah, Leon, dis me.' Dat when him close 'e eye an' start de rattle ... Kno' wuh dat is?*"

"*Oh yeah Sistuh, I kno' wuh de death rattle' is,*" the midwife says.

"*Well, Leon rattle some mo' b'fo' de Lawd teke him home ... buh I ent cry. I too num' to do dat. Dr. Johnson an' Mr. Fleming come back aftuh while, and Mr. Fleming ax me to go wid him. I walk out de room, en' turn and see Dr. Johnson pull de sheet obuh Big Leon head ... Dat when I cry.*"

Ella Mae stands and goes back into the bedroom to check on Charlotte and the baby. "*Wuh yah need?*" she asks Charlotte.

"*I thu'sty, Miss Ella Mae.*" Before the midwife can turn around, Mary is standing by the bed with water. Ella Mae picks up the baby and leaves the room while Mary wipes Charlotte's brow and gives her a cool drink.

"*Wan' sump'n to eat?*"

"*No, Momma. I jis thu'sty*"

Mary places a damp cloth on Charlotte's forehead. "*Alright chil', res' some mo' now.*

She joins Ella Mae, who is sitting in a chair in the front room holding the baby. Moments later Jacob walks in with his best friend, Arthur Givens.

"Good afuhnoon Miss Mary, Miss Ella Mae," Arthur says.

"Hello Arthur," the ladies say in unison. Mary motions for the boys to come see the baby. *"But don' touch."*

The boys lean in and look closely, but say nothing.

"OK, dat 'nuf lookin'," Mary says. *"Ya'll go on out now, I go change de baby."*

"Yes ma'am," Jacob says.

The midwife says to Mary: *"I ent see Arthur since de day 'e born, but I kno' dat him cause he got de long chin. All dem Givens got de long chin."*

"Dat fuh sho', Sustuh. All ob 'em look like dat … dey sho' do.

Moments later, Ella Mae asks, *"Anyway, when de tide up?"*

"Anudduh hour."

"OK. Now finish tellin' me 'bout Big Leon passing," the midwife says.

Mary continues: *"Well, Mr. Fleming tell Cuz'n Elijah to teke me back to Wadmalaw, an' say 'e go bring Big Leon to de house en de mornin'. By de time I get home dat aftuhnoon, eberybody waitin' in de house — muh sistuh, muh chillum, Big Leon uncle an' several cuz'n. De word get round fas'. Dey say Willie Russell go come in de mornin' wid de coolin' board fuh to lay out Big Leon in de front room. Willie go meke 'de casket too."*

Not long afterward, Ella Mae pulls out her watch, says the tide is almost high and that her husband, Thomas, surely was at the landing by now in his boat to take her home.

"Tom a good man 'cept when he sit round waitin' fuh de tide to change," Ella Mae says. *"Dat man hab no patience."*

"Uh huh," Mary says, *"Big Leon, Gawd bless 'e soul, de same way … ent never say nuttin' out loud, jis gimme dat look."*

The women point fingers at each other and laugh. Mary puts the shrimp and rice inside two tin canisters, and they walk out on the porch. The midwife says she'll be back in six weeks, and Mary calls out to the boys: *"Ya'll go wid Miss Ella Mae to the landing."*

"Yes ma'am," they say in unison.

"I tote yuh bag," Arthur tells the midwife, and all three leave as the sun slips behind the trees.

CHAPTER 5

Mary White was 17 and Big Leon Logan was 20 when they got married. Logan men were Wadmalaw fishermen. Big Leon owned his own boat and went to Charleston, where he worked offshore with a group of men known as the Colored Fisherman Crew, and returned home on weekends and during the winter. Leon Jr. followed in his father's wake. Mary worries about Leon Jr. working offshore even though he is a master fleet fisherman. Her youngest son, Peter, lives on Edisto Island and works for Mr. Fleming as a cattle driver and horse groomer. Anna, Mary's oldest child, is Jacob's mother. She is a widowed seamstress who lives and works in Charleston. Charlotte, the youngest, is a professional cook who is married to Benjamin Pringle, a dockworker in Charleston.

Starting at age five Charlotte stood by the wood stove and watched everything her mother did, and soon was helping her. She has been cooking on her own since becoming a teenager. Charlotte wants to move down the coast to Beaufort with Benjamin and their new daughter, and hopes to cook in the town's popular Gold Eagle restaurant.

Benjamin works on the Cooper River docks in Charleston, where he helps load cotton, tobacco and other dry goods. It's a dangerous job. Two of his fellow workers have drowned in the past year. He got word about his new baby from Mr. Sammy, who captains his twenty-foot-long wooden boat with oars and a single sail twice a week to and from Wadmalaw and Charleston. Benjamin wants to get to Wadmalaw soon to help with his daughter's naming ceremony. The trip from Charleston takes five to eight hours one way, depending on the wind and tide. Benjamin plans to ride down with Mr. Sammy, Anna, Leon Jr. and two Logan cousins.

Mary and Charlotte are in the bedroom talking about the baby's naming ceremony set for Saturday. It is a Gullah tradition in which infants are given their regular names along with African ones. Family and friends gather for the festivities and enjoy food and libations in honor of their ancestors as well as the newborn. A tree is later planted in honor of the infant along with the child's umbilical cord. Jacob returns to the house after feeding table scraps to Mary's sow and three pigs in a pen near the woods behind the house.

"Go outside an' wash yah hand," Mary tells him.

"Yes ma'am."

The setting sun is below the trees now and a stiff Atlantic breeze whirls through the branches. While Jacob washes his hands at the pump, his eyes follow swatches of gray moss swaying from the limbs of the huge live oak tree beside the house. It reminds him of the long whiskers that hang from Mr. Abe Washington's chin. The old man lives next to Wadmalaw's two-room schoolhouse and likes to sit on his porch and greet the children as they come and go.

Jacob often pulls moss from trees and spreads it along with pine needles on the floors of his grandmother's house. It offers a pleasant aroma while warding off bugs. Occasionally, Mary slips fresh moss inside her shoes, which she says lowers her blood pressure. Sometimes men use mules to haul wagonloads of moss to the county landing, where boatmen, including Mr. Sammy, buy it for resale as stuffing for pillows and mattresses in Charleston.

Jacob knows Mr. Sammy will soon arrive from the city along with his mother, whom he has not seen in months. Jacob looks forward to moving to Charleston to live with her and go to school. He enjoys her stories about the port city where people from all over the world live, work and visit; and how they look, talk and act differently from the islanders.

Jacob has been going to the island school and enjoys it, especially being with friends and cousins his age. He also likes his teacher, who stays on the island during the week and returns to her home in Charleston on weekends.

Jacob finishes washing his hands, dries them on his shirt and goes to the house where Charlotte and his grandmother are in the main room with the baby. He sits next to the infant, who is in a makeshift bed near the fireplace.

"Yah clean?" Mary asks.

"Yes ma'am."

Charlotte looks up at Jacob. *"Dey say yah help me when I habin' de baby."*

"Uh-huh. I de bes' help Nana and Miss Ella Mae ebuh hab," her nephew says.

Charlotte's smiles: *"Can't wait to see de look on Benny face tomorrow when him meet 'e dau'tuh."*

"Wuh you go name her?" Jacob asks.

"Sarah Mary Pringle — aftuh Benny's momma, Sarah, an' yuh Nana, Mary."

CHAPTER 6

It's dusk on Wadmalaw Island now and Mary lights an oil lamp on the table in the main room.

"Jacob, come git yah plate fuh suppuh," she says.

"Yes ma'am ... You go tell us a ghos' story later?" he asks.

"Not t'night," Mary says.

"I ent skay'd of dem story," Jacob vows.

"Dat cause yah spooky," Charlotte quips.

Mary serves everyone's plates. *"Tonight I go tell yah huh us git dis house, and yuh can pass 'um on to dis baby, who born right hey ..."*

Jacob and Charlotte smile as Mary continues:

"It been twenty-fo year since Big Leon get dis land from Mr. Fleming — ent cost much, tank Gawd an' tank Mr. Fleming too. Big Leon buil' de house quick. De soil good, an' close to de landing. So 'e stop fushin' in Chass'tun and work closer to home fuh Mr. Fleming."

"Huccome 'e stop fush'n' in Chass'tun?" Charlotte asked.

"Big Leon worry 'e gwine go out in dat ocean an' nebuh come back."

"Gran'daddy ebuh fall out de boat?" Jacob asks.

"Big Leon ent say cause 'e ent want me to worry 'bout dat ... Anyway, yah gran'daddy go all round hea' an' catch swimps, en crab, en fush an like dat. Him leeb b'fo de sun up an' stay way pas' dayclean. He sell de seafood to Mr. Fleming. Buh Big Leon wuh proud ob workin' wid de cullud Fush'men Crew in Chass'tun."

"Das why dey nickname him 'Big Fush,'" Charlotte says.

"Das right, an' dey call Leon Jr. 'Lil' Fush' cause he doin' wuh 'e daddy did. Nuttin' slow dat man down ... 'e work kin't to kin't."

"Kin't to kin't? Wuh dat mean?" Jacob asks.

"Dat mean 'e work from kin't see in de mornin' 'til kin't see at night. When Big Leon buil' dis house 'e spen' all day, all night an' all day a'gin an' a'gin workin' on it, an' 'e cuz'n he'p 'um. Dey meke the chimney wid crush oystuh shell mix up wid sand an' water. Dat wuh call 'tabby.' Dey also put de tabby on de cedar shake roof, an' some moss on top of dat, an' mix 'em good. House ent leak aftuh dey do all dat. Big Leon buil' de house on top of four big ol' cypress post in de ground ... cause cypress ent rot."

19

⦿ CHAPTER 7

Jacob awakes to the smell of bacon frying. Charlotte and Mary are in the kitchen talking and the baby is asleep in the bedroom. Jacob looks into the bedroom and sees his grandmother's little Bible open on the bed near the baby's head.

"Wuh yah doin' Jacob?" Mary asks.

"Why dat Bible in de bed, Nana?"

"I tell yah 'bout dat later. Git dress. Need mo' wood fuh de stobe."

"Alright Nana."

It's overcast and the wind blows steadily from the northeast as Jacob works up a sweat splitting short pieces of seasoned stove wood. He gathers an armful, brings it into to the house and puts it on the floor by the stove.

"Tank yuh, Jacob. I fix some egg while yuh go feed dem chicken. Brekwus be ready when yuh get back."

"Yes ma'am."

Mary fries two eggs over light to go with the bacon and boils some grits for Jacob while Charlotte dresses the baby.

"Momma, wuh yah tink de baby skin be like when her grow up? Charlotte asks. "I hope it stay light like Mr. Fleming daughtuh."

The Wadmalaw Logans typically have dark complexions — smooth and shiny like wet wood charcoal — with bright white teeth and wide brown eyes. Charlotte is self-conscious about the blackness of her own skin. She would rather it was the same tone as Lil' Sally Fleming, who was named after her grandmother. Charlotte has cooked for the Flemings at Moss Creek for several years.

"Why yah worry 'bout dat, Charlotte?" Mary asks.

"Mama, Lil' Sally skin look like sunshine b'fo' dark, an' her black hair long an' sleek. I want' muh chil' to look like dat," Charlotte says.

"Dat color call 'peola'," Mary says. "Some folk ent like 'um. Dey say peola people uppidy. Yah want yah chil' to be peola? Yuh want wan' her to hab skrait hair?"

"Momma, Benny fambly hab light skin an' scrait hair. Nuttin' wrong wid dat."

"Well ..." Mary says. "I ent wanna talk 'bout dat no mo'. I proud ob how us Logan look.

Mary fears change. She also fears Charlotte and her family will leave the island and never come back. That's because most of Charlotte's friends have moved to Charleston, Beaufort and Savannah. A few went to Philadelphia and New York City for better jobs. She walks out on the porch and hollers:

"Jacob! Come eat now."

"Yes ma'am."

After breakfast, Jacob takes the dishes outside and washes them at the handpump.

"Jacob, teke dem two bucket an' full 'em up wid water. Put one back by de stobe an' de oduh in de bedroom," Mary says. The bucket in the bedroom is used for washing up before going to bed.

"Yes ma'am."

Later he tells his grandmother that his friend Arthur Givens will be there soon, and they're going fishing in Rouse's Creek, a saltwater tributary of Bohicket Creek, which runs halfway across Wadmalaw.

"Yah done all I ax yah?"

"Yes ma'am."

"Wuh I tell yah 'bout goin' to dat crik?"

"You say if ent no grown-up down dey, I hab to come back home."

"Das right!"

Soon Arthur arrives with his cane pole and a bucket. Jacob hurries to the little shed where he keeps his fishing gear. The shed is next to the outhouse, a two-seater that Big Leon built. Rouse Creek is about a mile up the road past the schoolhouse.

As the boys are walking with their poles and fish bucket, Arthur says:

"De chimney in we house done fall in, Jacob."

"When?"

"Las' week aftuh dat big rain. We all stay in de front room now."

Jacob looks closely at Arthur's face to see if he's holding back a smile. Arthur is known for telling tales.

"Arthur, you ent lying is yah?"

"I tellin' de trute! Daddy an' Momma an' my brudduh an' sistuh an' me all sleepin' t'gethuh. Daddy go' fix de chimney, buh I ent kno' huh long dat go' teke."

"Nana say muh gran'daddy meke de chimney in our house," Jacob says. *"Big Leon buil' de house long time ago."*

"Huh 'e mek 'um?"

"Wid wide pine boa'ds, cypress logs an' oyshtuh shell."

"Shell? Dat don't sound right," Arthur says.

"No, boy, das de trute! He mixup shell wid sand an' water an' meke dat chimney, an' he put some ob dat tabby on de roof to full de crack."

Arthur shrugs, they laugh and keep walking until they see Mr. James, Mr. Green and Mr. Bunny near Tickle Up Bridge. The men are fishing and telling stories as usual.

The bridge has a high crest wide enough for one wagon at a time.

"Mornin' Mr. James, Mr. Green, Mr. Bunny," Jacob says.

The men look at the boys and Mr. James hollers, *"Who dat is?"*

"Dis Jacob an' Arthur."

"Great Gawd, ya'll done got so big yah look like bandit comin' to tief we fush, so us ready fuh fight," Mr. Bunny says as he wipes his forehead with a red bandana.

The men start laughing almost to tears, and the boys do too as Jacob slips over and peeks inside their fish bucket.

"Huh eberybody doin' wid dat new baby?" Mr. James asks Jacob.

"Dey, umm, good," he says as he tries to count the fish and talk at the same time.

Mr. James eyes Arthur. *"Huh yah momma and daddy, Arthur?"*

"Us need a new chimney ... de ol' one fall in all dat rain."

"Uh-huh. Tell yah daddy to go look at dat chimney at Jacob grandmother house b' fo' 'e try to meke a new one ... Dat ting solid, got de oyshtuh shell mix in."

Jacob and Arthur look at each other and smile.

"Looky hey, boys," Mr. Bunny says. *"I go' put a special worm on dis line and ketch ten fush at one time. I been lookin' round in de crik an' dey only eleben fush lef' down dey."*

Jacob leans over and whispers to Arthur. *"Mr. Bunny go ketch 'em all if we don' git busy."*

"Huh yuh know dat?" Arthur asks as he fumbles with his pole.

"He already got ten in de bucket ... I count 'em," Jacob whispers.

Two hours later, the boys have landed two croakers and five whitings while Mr. Bunny and his special worm got some nibbles but no fish. Jacob lays back on the bank with his pole in hand and recalls the time he rode over the bridge with his mother and grandmother just after dark while in the back of his cousin's wagon. Jacob recalls hearing the wheels clicking up the boards of the bridge then feeling a little tickle as the wagon rolled over the crest. He laughed, and his mother did too. When they reached the bottom of the bridge, the mule stopped and its ears stood straight up. Jacob heard a baby cry.

"Hush now chil' … Ebery'ting go be alright," he heard a woman' saying beneath the bridge. His cousin slapped the reins and the mule lurched forward. When they got to the house Jacob asked Mary and his mother if they heard anything when they stopped on the bridge. The women looked at each other and shrugged. Later that night when Jacob was almost asleep, he heard Anna and Mary talking as they sat at the kitchen table:

"I ent say nuttin' cause Jacob ent ol' 'nuf to kno' 'bout all dat," his grandmother said. *"Buh I tink 'e hea' spirrut unduh de bridge … I ent like crossin' dat bridge aftuh dark, 'specially if de wind blowin' hard down dat creek. It spooky."*

As rumor has it, one night before the bridge was built, a mother and her baby were in a canoe going down the creek after visiting with her lover, whose house was upstream. The canoe hit a stump and turned over about where the bridge was later built. The boat was found the next day upside down at the water's edge; the mother and child were not … ever. People say a conjureman from Charleston with eyes as red as the devil's had been hired by her lover's wife to put a hex on the woman — and that's what killed them … All of which Jacob was thinking about when he heard Arthur yelling: *"Jacob! Jacob! Wake up, boy! Yuh gotta fush. Oooh, dat a big one … pull 'um in!"*

Jacob scrambles to his feet and grabs his fishing pole, which is bent double. That's when Jacob heaves back on the pole and up came a flounder big and round as a sweetgrass doormat. Jacob falls backward onto the bank and his catch landes beside him flapping like a fish out of water, which it was.

"Dat a whopp'uh!" Mr. Bunny hollers.

Jacob rolls over and grabs the snaggle-tooth fish with one hand by its gills and sits up proudly. The fish, which has two eyes on the same side of its head but none on the bottom, stares straight at him.

Tha's when the sky darkens and thunder rolls in on clouds off the Atlantic. Jacob drops the fish in the boys' bucket, and everyone gathers their things and skeedaddles. The boys take turns carrying the heavy bucket to the house, where Mary waits on the porch.

"I glad yah got back befo' de rain and lightnin'," she holleres. *"Wuh yah got in dat bucket?"*

CHAPTER 8

The next morning Jacob and his grandmother are up before daybreak preparing for Benjamin's afternoon arrival from Charleston. Meanwhile, Benjamin, who works on the docks of the port city and stays in an East Side tenement house, finishes stuffing his canvas bag with food, clothing, medicines, toiletries, newspapers and gifts. He walks across town to the Ashley River wharf, where Mr. Sammy is waiting in his boat for the trip to Wadmalaw. They shove off as the sun rises over Charleston.

Benjamin takes a seat in the bow and Mr. Sammy rows across the mouth of the Ashley River into Wappoo Creek. They ride the incoming tide until they get to Elliott's Cut where the boat picks up speed as the water flows quickly into the Stono River. Sammy raises the sail and off they go to Wadmalaw. Gulls that have been following the boat on high suddenly swoop down low around the men. Benjamin smiles, looks back and sees Sammy manning the sail and rudder while throwing pieces of cornbread out for the birds.

"Yah been mighty quiet Benny," Sammy says. *"Now dat I hab yah 'tention, yah wanna talk 'bout wuh on yah mind?"*

"Been tinkin' 'bout money," Benjamin says. *"Charlotte and the baby stay on Wadmalaw cause it cost too much fuh dem to libe wid me in Chass'tun. I tinkin' 'bout goin' to Bew'fut and work in de lumbuh-ya'd down dey."*

"Uh-huh," Sammy says. *"Do Charlotte kno' 'bout dat?"*

"Oh yeah, her kno', and she happy 'cause us a fambly now, yah kno'."

"Uh-huh," I glad to hea' dat."

It's early afternoon as Jacob leaves the house and walks to Tickle Up Bridge to rendezvous with Mr. James and his cousin Emma, who are waiting with horse and wagon at the landing for Benjamin's arrival. Emma lives on Wadmalaw and is two years older than Jacob. They are more like siblings than cousins. She is protective of Jacob, and knows he was born with the veil.

After sailing for almost nine hours, Sammy's boat rounds a bend in Bohicket Creek and heads for the landing. Benjamin hears someone calling from the shore and stands up in the bow:

"Benny Pringle, das you?"

"Who dat?" Benjamin yells back.

"Dis James Weston. I teke yah to Mary house."

"Hey Cuz'n Benny," Emma calls out from the back of the wagon. *"Yah a daddy now! Huh dat feel?"*

"I ent kno'," Benjamin yells back. *"I tell yuh later."*

Mr. James climbs down from his rig, walks up to Jimey, his horse, rubs the animal's nose and feeds him a carrot. The boat slips onto shore and Benjamin gets out. Emma runs to the water's edge, grabs Benjamin's duffle bag and totes it up to the wagon. Benjamin thanks Sammy, hands him a couple of dollars and hurries up the bank to help Emma with the big bag.

"Dat ting heaby, girl, I teke 'um res' ob de way," he says.

She runs to the wagon, climbs in the back and says, *"Han' dat ting up to me old man Bennie. Yah a daddy now ... yah go need yah res'."*

Benjamin laughs, gives the bag to Emma and takes a seat next to Mr. James.

"Benny, yah lookin' good," James says. *"Gimmie some a dat,"* he adds as he grabs Benjamin's muscular arm.

"Still workin' dem dock," Benjamin says, then turns to Emma. *"Lil' Cuz, yah all gro' up now, an' purty too."*

Emma smiles, leans back against his duffle bag and off they go. She eyes the live oaks and limbs festooned with long, gray moss as the wagon passes under the trees. She reaches up, grabs handfuls of the beardlike bromeliad and piles it beside her.

"Benjamin," James says after a while, *"I got de spirrut name fuh yah baby buh ent go say 'um now."*

"I ent mind waitin'," Benjamin says with a big smile.

When they arrive at the bridge, James slows Jimey to a stop.

Jacob, who is sitting under a mulberry tree on the other side of the creek, stands up: *"Hey y'all! I obuh hey!"*

Emma ducks down so Jacob can't see her. James tells Jimey to proceed and the wagon crosses over the bridge to the other side of the creek. He pulls back the reins and stops next to Jacob.

"Hello Jacob," Mr. James says.

Benjamin jumps down, shakes the boy's hand and gives him a bear hug. Jacob smiles broadly when Emma jumps up, dumps an armful of moss on his head and leaps on the boy's back. They fall into the grass and Emma starts tickling him. After the tickling stops, they brush themselves off. Still laughing, they climb into the back of the rig, Benjamin joins Mr. James on the front seat and the wagon continues to the house. As they roll into the yard, they see Mary waving from the porch. The wagon stops, everyone gets out and James ties Jimey to a tree. He gives the horse an apple, grabs an empty bucket and goes to the porch pump to get the animal some water. Jacob and Emma unload the duffle bag while Benjamin hurries inside.

Charlotte, who is in the bedroom, leans over the cradle and tucks the baby in, then steps into the front room. Benjamin kisses her forehead. He lifts her head, looks into her eyes and gently wipes away her tears.

"I hey now, so dry dem eye," he tells his wife.

"Benny, you ent know huh much I miss yuh. I all mix up fuh while, buh happy now cause yah wid me ... Now, looky wuh I got fuh yuh." Charlotte grabs her husband's hand and they go into the bedroom. Benjamin looks inside the cradle, lifts his tiny daughter, holds her to his chest and rocks from side to side.

"Dis yah daddy," Benjamin whispers. *"I go' teke care a yah, an' yah momma too."*

Mr. James carries the water back to Jimey, dips a brush in the bucket and strokes the horse's neck, chest and sides. He climbs onto the wagon seat and tells everyone goodbye. Mary asks him to stay and eat.

"Ent got no time, Mary. I be back t'morruh fuh de ceremony."

"OK, James, and tank yah!" Mary says as Emma wraps her arms around her waist. Mary turns and removes bits of moss from Emma's hair and shirt. *"Drag dat bag obuh dey,"* she says and points to the front corner near the bedroom door.

Not long afterward, Benjamin has unpacked his things in the bedroom and sits in the main room with Charlotte while the baby feeds at her mother's breast.

"Charlotte, I bet yah wondrin' wuh in muh bag. I saw yah lookin'."

"Wuh yuh bring me?" she asks.

The baby is asleep now so Charlotte puts her down in the bedroom. She places Mary's pocketsize Bible above the child's head and opens the book to the 23rd Psalm. She pulls some thin white netting across the top of the crib to keep out mosquitoes.

Jacob watches his aunt and the baby, turns to his grandmother and asks, *"Is yah go tell me now why dat little Bible in de bed wid her?"*

"Uh-huh, I tell yah now," Mary says. *"Us open 'um to the 23rd Psalm an' put 'um dey to scay de nasty old 'hag' away frum dis place. Ent need nutt'n like dat*

round hey fuh sho'."

"I ent 'fraid ob no hag," Jacob says. *"I go look out fuh little Sarah too."*

Charlotte leaves the baby with the door open slightly, hurries across the main room and sits beside Benjamin, who reaches behind his back and pulls out a big paper bag. She reaches in and pulls out a light blue, cotton dress with white frills at the bottom. She stands, holds it up to check the size and gently folds it across her arm. She leans over and kisses him on the cheek.

"Tank yah Benny. Dat bootiful!" She reaches into the bag again and pulls out another dress, which is light brown with blue trim. *"How yah find two purty dress like dis fuh me?"*

Benjamin smiles broadly. *"Anna pick 'em out."*

"I ent hab no store-bought dress b'fo'," Charlotte says.

He hands her a smaller bag. She reaches in and removes two tiny dresses — one pink, the other white. *Baby go' look good in these … Benjamin Pringle, you a good man. Us bless to hab yah."*

"I bless too," he says, stands up, walks to the kitchen area and hands another bag to his mother-in-law.

"Wuh dis?" Mary asks and dries her hands on a towel. She opens the bag and pulls out pound of Prince Albert tobacco in the can. *"Benny, huh yah kno' I ent got no 'bacca? I go' sit on de po'ch aftuh suppuh an' smoke 'um."*

"Look in dat bag some mo'," he says.

She reaches in and pulls out two more tins, one a pound of ground coffee and the other full of crushed, black tea leaves. Mary slaps the table, laughs and laughs some more. *"I ent hab no coffee, an' no tea too. Somebody told yah dat?"*

Benjamin smiles broadly. *"No ma'am. I jis' bring 'em fuh yah."*

Next, she pulls out two paper-wrapped bars of scented soap.

"Tank yuh, tank yuh, tank yuh!" she says as tears well up in her eyes.

Benjamin walks back to his chair, grabs another bag and hands it to Emma. She reaches in and pulls out a blue and white linen scarf. *"Oooo, dat nice, Bennie. I go wear dis tomorruh at de ceremony."* Benjamin hands a small bag to Jacob, who looks inside and smiles. He got several sinkers and box of fishing hooks.

Later, after supper, everyone except Mary settled in for the night. She sat in her porch rocker and lit her pipe then heard the door open behind her. *"I couldn't fall asleep, Nana,"* Jacob said as he sat in a chair next to his grandmother.

"Wuh wrong Jacob?"

"I been tinkin' 'bout dat nasty hag," Jacob said. *"Emma say a hag ol' and skinny; dat she slip in de house when eberybody sleepin', an' latch on to yah and suck de breath out yah, and dey like dat on babies de bes'."*

"Well, Jacob, dat wuh de ol' folk say. I ent nebuh see no hag, buh ent go teke no chance wid dat baby in de house. Das why I open muh Bible jis right and lay 'um side dat chil'. Gawd look out fuh her."

 # CHAPTER 9

It's Friday morning in downtown Charleston. Anna Rouse is up and dressed at 5 a.m. for the day-long boat ride to Wadmalaw Island. She made sandwiches for Mr. Sammy, Leon Jr. and herself, and packed her suitcase the night before. She leaves her crowded tenement and waits at St. Michael's Church at the corner of Meeting and King streets for her brother, who lives several blocks north.

Leon Jr. is on the porch of his place wrapping 15 pounds of fresh shrimp in thick brown paper. His wife, Hazel, brings out his packed duffle bag and wishes him a safe trip. He lifts his bag and straps it across his shoulder and back, slips the wrapped seafood inside a canvas carry sack and walks over to Meeting Street and down several blocks to Broad Street to where Anna is waiting. From there it's a short walk west to the Ashley River wharf.

"Morning, Anna," he calls out when he sees his sister waiting in the glow of a street lamp. *"We gotta hurry … tide low and 'bout to change. Hope yah packed light. Mr. Sammy go be waitin …"*

They walk past several vegetable vendors who have filled their carts with fresh produce grown across Wappoo Creek on James Island. When they reach the docks Leon Jr. spots Sammy waiting in boat, which is flanked by small wooden boats loaded with fresh vegetables.

"Hello, Mr. Sammy, yah doin' OK?" Leon Jr. says. Sammy smiles, greets Anna and Leon, and loads their gear into the boat.

"Ya'll hurry on board, tide leavin' soon," Sammy says. *"Anna, sit in de bow wid dat big bucket. I got some block ice fuh yah bruddah. Leon, sit in de middle, and pull dem oar when we need 'em. I got the rudder and de sail."* Leon puts the fresh seafood on ice. The wind picks up slightly and off they sail across

the Ashley into the fast-flowing waters of Wappoo Creek through Elliott's Cut and into the Stono River.

The sun is all the way up now, Anna looks past Leon Jr. to the stern and asks, *"Mr. Sammy, you been mekin' dis run fuh long as I 'membuh ... yah 'bout ready to retire?"*

No, Anna, not til the Lawd teke me home ... and only Him know huh long dat go' be."

"Amen," Leon adds.

Anna is reminded of her husband, Edward Rouse, who drowned six months after Jacob was born, and her own father, Big Leon Logan, who died a month later. She has yet to understand why God wanted it that way.

The wind stops. Leon lifts the oars and rows up the Stono River.

Moments later, Sammy asks, *"Anna, wuh yah tinkin' 'bout?"* Which is what he always asks his passengers.

"Tinkin' 'bout seein' eberybody, 'specially Jacob an' de baby."

"Uh-huh. I glad yah fambly go' name dat newborn twice like de ol' folk do. Lot'a young people ent do dat no mo'."

"Ting changin'," she replies. *"Ent many elder lef' to keep 'em skrait. An' city folk ent care 'bout nuttin like dat."*

Sammy agrees. *"Dem ol' folk ent go be round hey fuh'ebuh. It up to you an' Leon an' all now to 'membuh wey yah from ... If young folk ent kno' it, dey loss'."*

Sammy steers the boat past Johns Island toward Wadmalaw Sound. The wind picks up again, Benjamin stops rowing and up goes the sail. Sammy maneuvers the craft through the white foam and the river chop while Anna holds her hand off the side and down into the bubbles. Sammy looks at Leon Jr. and asks, *"Hey, Lil Fush, wuh all in dat ice bucket?"*

"Fufteen pound a swimps and some black bass ... Caught 'em yesterday."

"Sistuh Mary go' be glad 'bout dat," Mr. Sammy says.

After a while, the old captain starts singing, which is customary when under sail. *"Lawd, I wanna be a Christian. Lawd, I wanna be a Christian — in my heart, in my heart ..."* Leon Jr. soon joins in and Anna hums while the boat glides through the open waters of the sound.

⬤CHAPTER 10

Benjamin left Wadmalaw earlier that morning from the Bohicket Creek landing to visit with his family on Johns Island. He planned to return to Mary's house that afternoon in time for the arrival of Leon Jr. and Anna.

Emma and Jacob feed the chickens and hogs, and carry water in buckets from the pump to Mary's vegetable garden on the sunny side of the house. Jacob didn't sleep much the night before in anticipation of seeing his mother. He dreamed intermittently that he had been talking to her. When he told Emma about this, she laughed and pinched him on the arm in jest. Jacob doesn't usually talk about his dreams except when he's with Emma.

It's late in the afternoon now and the tide is high as Sammy's boat arrives at the landing. Mr. James is waiting there with his horse, Jimey, and the wagon. Leon Jr. and Anna load everything in the back, including their bags and the bucket full of fresh shrimp and fish on ice. Leon Jr. pays Sammy, and soon he, Anna, James and Jimey are off to Mary's house. After a while, James says:

"Sho' be nice when ya'll move back to Wadmalaw…"

Nobody says anything in response.

"Ya'll comin' back some day, ent yah?"

Leon Jr. sits up straight and says:

"Now dis me talkin'… I ent kno' 'bout Anna. Buh muh wife, Hazel, ent go lib hey… Her a city gal. Ent no way she lib on Wadmalaw. She scay'd ob water too."

"Huh 'bout you, Anna?" Mr. James asks.

"Well, I got work in de city, an' Jacob need to go to school in Chass'tun."

Mr. James, looking straight ahead, nods his head. *"They wuh boff yah sayin'. Jis 'membuh wey yah come from. Don' nebuh fuhgit dat!"*

Anna removes her scarf, and the men admire her hair, which is neatly braided front to back with a little blue latch at the tip end. Leon takes off his jacket and rolls up the sleeves of his brown plaid flannel shirt to his elbows. They cross Tickle-Up Bridge, James pulls back on the reins and stops the wagon on the other side of the creek. Leon Jr. jumps down to clear the road of large broken oak limb.

Anna watches the water flow swiftly under the bridge and remembers when she, her mother and Jacob crossed years ago. That was when Jacob said he heard a baby crying, although nobody else did. She worries about Jacob — who reminds her of Big Leon. She remembers what some elders were talking about following her husband's funeral, when folks like him die, their spirits return when a baby joins the family.

"Jacob sho' seem like a ol' man sometime," she whispers to herself. *"Wonduh wuh de Lawd got plan fuh dat boy?"*

Leon Jr. clears the limb and returns to the wagon. When they arrive at the house, Mary is on the porch. She's wearing a plain dress, a white cotton scarf on her head and a dark blue apron around her waist. Charlotte steps out with the baby in her arms. Jacob and Emma scamper from around the sunny side of the house to greet everyone.

"Slow down, ya'll go spook dat hoss," Mary warns.

Mr. James helps Anna down from the wagon and Jacob gives his mother a bear hug without saying a word.

"Help yah Uncle Leon bring eberyting in," she tells him.

"Hey Momma," Anna says when she gets to the porch. Mary wraps her arms around her daughter. *"Muh sweet Annie, huh yah do?"*

"I alrigh'."

"Now I hab all my chillum unduh de same roof," Mary smiles and says.

Anna kisses her sister Charlotte on the cheek, and asks, *"Wuh dat yah holdin'?"*

"Dis yah niece." Charlotte hands the baby to Anna.

"Great Gawd!" Anna says. *"She purty like her momma."*

Meanwhile, Emma pumps a bucketful of water and Jacob carries it to Mr. James, who sets it down for Jimey to drink. James hands Jacob a brush and asks him to give Jimey a good rub down. After that Mr. James climbs back on board and lifts the reins.

"See yah t'morruh!" he says.

 **CHAPTER 11**

Everyone is sitting in the front room now and Anna marvels at how much Jacob has grown. *"Wuh Nana feedin' you?"*

"Eberyting her gimme," Jacob says, and everyone laughs.

"Jacob sta'tin' to look like Big Leon, Gawd bless 'e soul," Leon Jr. says.

Jacob listens quietly while his mother senses he wants to say something.

"Wuh wrong, Jacob?" she asks.

"You an' Uncle Leon ent talk right," Jacob says.

Anna smiles. *"Dat 'cause white folk en Chass'tun ent unduhstan' wuh us be sayin' so we change how we talk a little.*

"Das right," Leon Jr. adds. *"Some dem buckra say I should quit talkin' Gullah."*

"Uh, huh," Anna says. *"Dat wuh call 'goin' in an' out' — when yah talk to de buckra one way an' yah talk like us doin' now to each oduh. Now, some cullud folk in Chass'tun ent use Gullah no mo'. Dey talk like de buckra all de time — eberyting get all mix up. Anyway, aftuh all dis gwine in an' gwine out, yah Uncle an' me ent always talk like us did be' fo' an' don' eben kno' it."*

Jacob shrugs his shoulders. *"Wuh dey call dat buckra talk in Chass'tun?"*

"English," Leon Jr. says, with a smile.

"Our teacher talk like dat. Her frum Chass'tun," Emma says.

Anna nods. *"You an' Jacob go' talk like dat too someday."*

CHAPTER 12

It's dark outside when Benjamin gets back to Mary's house. *"Smell like I jis' in time fuh suppuh,"* he says as he opens the porch door and steps into the main room.

"Yah sho' is," Mary says as she takes the cornbread out of the stove. *"OK ya'll, eberybody is hey and food on de table. Time to say grace."*

They hold hands and Benjamin asks the blessing over fried chicken, rice with gravy and turnip greens. Everyone fills their plates and sits in the living area. Afterwards, Leon Jr., Charlotte and Emma go onto the porch. Leon says to Emma:

"I ent neber see so much white people in one place aftuh I move to Chass'tun. Some dem buckra be nice, some ent. Some talk to yah, some don'."

Benjamin sits at the table next to Anna and thinks about how much better it would have been if Hazel was there. Mary settles in on the sofa. *"Peter comin' tomorrow from Edisto; Mamie go be hey too,"* she says.

Mary worries about her youngest son. Before marrying Mamie Robinson two years ago, she told Peter she didn't think it was a good match, but never said why. Peter already knew:

Mamie's father dabbled in a dangerous form of folk medicine. People on Edisto said he was associated with a treacherous "root doctor." Rumor had it that after Mr. Robinson learned that Peter Logan wanted to marry his daughter he visited the notorious conjureman with red eyes from Charleston. According to rumor, Mr. Robinson paid the conjureman to "put a root" on his own daughter so she couldn't have children. Then he told Peter about the root, warning him he had better change his mind about marrying Mamie. Peter married her anyway. The rumor mill caught fire after she became pregnant and had a miscarriage. She was with child a second time and lost that one too.

After supper, Jacob and Emma put the used pots, pans, dishes and tableware in the washtub and carried it out to the pump. That's when Mary reached in the cupboard, grabbed her pipe and her can of Prince Albert and sat in her porch rocker. After she packed her pipe and lit up, Leon Jr. stepped out on the porch saying, *"Dat smell good, Momma. Weh yuh git dat 'bacca?"*

"Benny bring 'um."

"I glad him did dat fuh yuh," Leon says.

Mary chuckles. *"Me too, cause if he ent, I put either you an' Benny on dat boat an' meke yah go back an' get 'um."*

They laugh.

"Momma," Leon Jr. says, *"I sorry Hazel ent come wid me again. She hab to help her uncle at de lumbuh-ya'd."*

Mary knows Leon Jr. is making yet another excuse for his wife. She puffs twice on her pipe and says, *"Hazel a grown 'ooman dat kin do wuh her wanna do."* Mary takes two more puffs. *"Jis 'membuh wey yah come from an' who yuh fambly be — das wuh mattuh mos' to me."*

# CHAPTER 13

Mary and Anna are up early the next morning to prepare for the big meal that afternoon. Emma is asleep on the floor in the bedroom with Charlotte, Benjamin and the baby. The sky is clear with a slight breeze outside. Benjamin, Leon Jr. and Jacob are out back setting up the pit over which they will roast hog meat, chickens and fish. Jacob sees a tall man out front on the road. *"Hey come Uncle Peter,"* he says.

Peter, the youngest of the Logan siblings, is the tallest at six feet. He is muscular, bald with a dark complexion. Beads of sweat often form on the top of his head and run down his brow. He is a master carpenter with a booming voice and hardy laugh.

"Hello," Peter bellows as he walks up on the porch. *"Anybody home?"*

Mary smiles broadly and says, *"Boy, if you don' git on in dis house, I go come out dey an' put yah 'cross my lap an' gib yah a beatin'."*

Charlotte and Anna laugh as Peter puts his bags down and hugs his mother. *"Weh my new niece?"*

"In de bedroom wid Emma," Charlotte says.

Peter goes into the back room where Emma stands and hugs him. *"Missy Emma, yah is sproutin' like a gum tree,"* he says in a much lower voice. He looks at the baby, who is asleep, and slowly pulls back the netting. He strokes her cheeks gently, touches her forehead and smiles, wishing he had a child of his own.

He returns to the front room and says, *"Sis, I happy fuh yuh. Dat a purty baby."*

"Tank yuh Petee," Charlotte says.

"Huh Mamie doin'?" Mary asks.

Peter sits at the table. *"Her sick again. One week her feelin' good; de nex' week she sick."* He rubs his head and continues. *"Doc Johnson been seein' Mamie, and say 'e go check on her 'gain nex' mont' ... I ent kno' wuh mo' 'e can do."*

Mary listens carefully. She doesn't know if Charlotte and Anna have heard the rumor about Mamie's root, and she's convinced that Dr. Johnson cannot help her daughter-in-law if it is true. She continues:

"Son, befo' yuh go home, grab some leaf off muh peach tree. When yah get dey, soak 'em in water fuh a hour an' let 'em dry. Put dem leaf on she fo' head an' her ches' an' boff she leg. Den put a pan a water unduh de bed an' keep 'um dey. Meke sho her keep dem leaf on fuh three hour. Uh-huh. Dat draw de febuh from she body and into de pan."

"OK Momma. I go do dat," Peter says. *"Ent nobody in Mamie fambly say nutt'n 'bout wuh wrong wid she. Momma, you bin right when yah tell me dem Robinson be strange. I see dat now."*

Mary places her hands up on her son's broad shoulders. *"Stay skrong son.*

Hab fait' in de Lawd and eberyting go' work out… He go help get dat root off Mamie. Hey wuh I sayin'?"

"Yes ma'am," Peter says. He stands and goes out back to help set up the cooking pit. He removes his outer shirt and hangs it on a limb. Still wearing his sleeveless thick grey undershirt, he walks back to the pit feeling a little better than before.

Mary picks up her paring knife and cuts up okra from the garden.

"Momma," Charlotte whispers. *"Who put de root on Mamie."*

Mary turns and looks at her daughters. *"I nebuh hey nutt'n 'bout dat,"* she lies. *"Buh I do got sump'n to say dat I ent want nobody else to kno'. Yuh hey me girls?"*

Both Charlotte and Anna nod.

"B' fo' Peter marry dat gal, I tell 'um Mr. Robinson all mix up wid de root, an' mos' folk on Edisto kno' dat. Dey go see Robinson when dey wanna fix somebody good or fix 'um bad. I tell Peter don' marry Mamie, and if yah Daddy bin livin',' him would say same ting… Mamie ent hab no chillum cause a conjureman put a root down on she, an' 'til her git dat ting off, dey ent go be no chillum fuh sho'."

Anna and Charlotte promise their mother that they won't say anything to anyone else about what they just heard.

 **CHAPTER 14**

For special occasions such as naming ceremonies for Gullah newborns, island men typically get up before sunrise and slow roast a whole hog, chickens, fish and cuts of fresh venison on a wide metal sheet placed over wood coals in an open pit. The Logans are no exception. It's Saturday afternoon in the woods behind Mary's house. The hog is split down the middle and halved chickens sizzle atop a sheet of tin over hickory and oak coals.

"OK, das it fuh now," says Leon Jr., the family pit master, an honor he inherited from his father. *"We'll put dem swimps on later."*

Mary, Emma and the other ladies have finished in the kitchen and are changing clothes for the festivities. The women will wear white dresses and tie their hair back off their foreheads with white linen scarfs.

Mr. James, who has chosen a spiritual name for the child, and his wife are expected to arrive before dark along with various aunts, cousins and nephews.

This duty of selecting the spiritual name has been passed down to Mr. James because of his age and knowledge of Gullah ways.

The sun is almost down and an autumn breeze rustles the leaves. Jacob and his uncles have changed into white shirts, dress pants and Sunday shoes, and wait outside near the porch for the guests. Mary, Anna and Emma will come outside soon followed by Charlotte and the baby. If the child had been born in winter, a smaller ceremony would take place inside the house, and the big meal would follow in the spring.

It was almost dark when Mr. James, his family and the others rounded the bend in his wagon and rolled to a stop in Mary's yard. They share pleasantries with the men, who help the women down from the wagon. Mary and her family members exit the house, and everyone walks together down the path into the woods. They assemble around the fire pit, which is illuminated by "fat lighter" torches. "Fat lighter" is easily ignitable resin-filled longleaf pinewood. The meats are simmering now and Jacob's stomach growls. He adds a couple of hickory logs to the coals.

Charlotte, in a white dress with long sleeves, stands holding her baby close to her chest and Emma is beside her in case she needs help with the child. Benjamin stands on the other side of Charlotte. The baby is wearing a beautiful white linen dress and matching bonnet, both of which Anna made in Charleston. Mr. James, decked out in long, white vestments and a broad straw hat, raises his hands.

"Silence, please!" he says and everyone quiets down. The leaves continue to rattle in the breeze and the wood crackles in the pit. Mr. James continues, *"Us hey dis ebnin' to honor dis man an' dis 'ooman wuh hab dis chil' dat come into de worl' seben day ago. Dis baby is one wid most ob us in de blood, an' some ob us in de spirrut, as we gathuh round t'night. Dis chil' go git two name during dis ceremony. Dat wuh our people been doing fuh a long, long time."*

Mr. James pauses, turns to Charlotte and gently lifts the baby from her arms. *"Wuh name you gib' dis chil'?"* he asks Charlotte and Benjamin, who leans over and whispers in Mr. James's left ear. He nods and says, *"Benjamin an' Charlotte name dis chil' Sarah Mary Pringle."* Everyone smiles and claps.

"Hold on, ya'll, hold on," Mr. James says, *"I go gib Sarah she spirrut name nex' ... All ob us hey t'night kno 'bout dis cause us all done got our spirrut name... an' us mus' 'membuh 'um cause dat who us go be when we reach de oduh side, praise Gawd!"*

Everyone nods and whispers their spirit names to each other. Mr. James waits a few moments, raises his hand and declares, *"I name dis chil' Kiesee… Dat mean 'joy an' good fortune'."*

Everyone smiles and claps some more as he kisses Sarah/*Kiesee* on both cheeks before passing her back to her mother.

Next, Benjamin gives a pitcher of water to Mr. James, who holds it up so everyone can see it. *"Dis water bin bless by de elders, an' am libation fuh de spirrut an' to all ob dem dat gon' b'fo'."* He calls out the spiritual names of family members and friends from the islands who have passed away as he pours a little water on the ground, then sprinkles what's left on all the living who have gathered there. Jacob remembers Leon Sr.'s name, *Rashidi*, which means "good counsel," and Mary's name, *Balinda*, for "patience, endurance and fortitude." His mother, Anna, is *Anaya*, or "one who looks up to God."

Jacob's spiritual name is *Moyo Samba*, which means "spirit life and merciful." He knows about the veil and that his birthmark, a natural amulet, protects him and represents a continuation of life.

Mr. James asks Mary to speak next, so she steps forward and says:

"I's so happy, so full up wid joy dis evenin' dat I got my fambly an' friend hey. I talkin' to yah now through Leon Sr., who lookin' down an' smilin'. Him say he proud an' dat he 'membuh wey him come from… He say alway 'membuh yah people, an' yah go be on de right path.' He say de blood Gawd put in we vein is dey fuh good reason… an' dat each ob we kno' wuh dat is as long as us seek de trute. Buh him say de trute ent alway easy to find … dat de wey Gawd mean fuh 'um to be."

Mary pauses for a moment to keep from crying.

"Das alrigh', Mary, teke yuh time," Mr. James says as Benjamin wraps his right arm around his mother-in-law. She takes a big breath and continues:

"I tell all my chillum dat eberyting changin' fas', an' I know yah wanna see wuh all out dey in de wurl'. I axe dat when you do, don' fuhgit to keep Gawd in yah heart, and if yah do, yah find wuh yah lookin' for… I done now, time to eat."

Mary turns around, lifts her arms skyward and praises God as she walks up the path, onto the porch and back inside the house with Charlotte and baby Sarah close behind her. The other ladies socialize briefly before going to the house, change their clothes and return to the kitchen area and front room. The men step behind the house and quickly change before going back to the pit. Jacob grabs an empty fruit jar with holes in the lid and chases lightning bugs around the yard. The insects actually blink green as they fly. He grabs them one by one and drops them into the jar. His younger cousins grab some and put them in the jar too.

The men have set up two long tables not far from the pit. Earlier in the day they had placed a metal sheet over the coals and laid out seasoned cuts of chicken and venison alongside the split hog — all of which has been slow-cooked to perfection. Now Jacob's flounder goes on, followed by the sea bass. The fish stay on until crispy. The shrimp are last, and cook fast. The women return and set the tables with glasses, plates and utensils, then bring out various side dishes from the kitchen along with slices of bread and whole pies they had baked earlier inside Mary's stove. Leon Jr. places cuts of the meats and the seafood on the table and asks Mr. James to say the blessing.

Such festive occasions are similar on South Carolina's sea islands for weddings, wakes and Memorial Day celebrations. The meats are served with sweet-potato pone, stewed tomatoes, okra, cornbread, collard greens, rice and beans, shrimp, cakes, cobblers, bread pudding and pies. After the blessing, everyone sits down, digs in and enjoys each other's company.

"Wey de man who ketch dis big ol' flounda' I gittin' ready to teke off de fiah?" Peter asks.

"Dat de bigges' flounda' I eber see," Leon Jr. adds.

Jacob places the jar of captured fireflies on the ground and examines his cooked fish. *"I de one dat ketch 'um,"* he says proudly.

"Boy, hush yuh mout!" Peter says. *"Ent no wey yah ketch a fush dat big. Yuh gotta be a skrong man like Uncle Benny to do dat."*

"A big ol' fush like dat pull a boy in de water an' beat 'um wid 'e tail," Benjamin pipes in.

Jacob scratches his head and says, *"I ketch dat fush, axe Mr. James an' Arthur. Dey bin dey, an' dey ent go lie!"*

The men are all laughing when Leon Jr. says, *"Big, bad Jacob ketch dat fush,"* then he grabs his nephew with one arm and tickles him until the boy manages to wiggle himself loose.

Then Emma pinches Jacob on his arm as she often does when she thinks his ego gets too big. The children finish eating and leave to play hide-and-seek. Cousin Purvis is it. Jacob hides in some bushes near the fig tree.

CHAPTER 15

"… Eight, nine, ten… ready or not, hey I come!" Cousin Purvis yells.

Jacob squats as low as he can under the fig tree and peeks through the branches to see who's coming. All is quiet now, except for a strange breeze on which Jacob thinks hears a voice: *"He'p me … Please he'p me!"*

Jacob turns around but sees no one. *"Weh you at?"* Jacob asks. He wants to run, but his feet are too heavy to move. Several voices surround him now. Something rubs across the back of his neck and hands pull on his shoulders. Jacob's feet and ankles turn cold as the voices get louder. His legs tingle as if ants are crawling on them. The voices fade, and what feels like a gust of warm air blows down his neck. Jacob closes his eyes, clinches his fists and waits for the worst. But nothing happens.

He opens his eyes and the voices return. Jacob rolls out from under the tree and stops face down on the ground. Sweat flows from his forehead and into his eyes. He struggles to catch his breath. And then …

"Tag! You it, Jacob!" Purvis screams in his left ear.

Jacob gets up and staggers across the yard to where the others have gathered for the next round.

"Wuh wrong Jacob?" Emma asks.

He stares at her, his face and shirt collar sopping wet.

"Wuh wrong?" she asks again.

"I hea' voices an' feel 'em touchin' me when I hidin' 'unduh dat fig tree," he whispers.

Emma grabs Jacob with one hand and pulls him away from the other children, then wipes sweat from his face and forehead. *"Jacob, dey say you got de gif', dat you see an' hea' ting nobody see or hea'."*

"So?" he replies.

"So why you unduh dat tree?" Emma asks. *"Nana say dat weh de spirrut be at."*

"I kno' dat … I ent skay'd ob no spirrut."

"Dat why you de one wid de gif'," she says. *"I glad I ent see 'em or hea' 'em cause dey dead,"* she says. *"You spooky!"* she adds with a smile and softly pinches his ear.

"Wuh ya'll up to?" says Mary, who surprises them. *"Y'all tusslin' agin? Go on obuh dey wid the other chillum an' mind yuh'self."*

"Yes ma'am," Jacob and Emma say in unison.

# CHAPTER 16

I t's early Sunday morning, and Mary has served a breakfast of fresh eggs, cured ham and grits with red-eye gravy. Most of the family is dressed and ready to walk a mile up the road and around the second bend to New Hope Baptist Church, a one-story building made of hand-hewn pine with a bell and a cedar-shake roof. It was built in the late 1800s, a sanctuary for all God's children as well as the Holy Ghost, according to the preacher, the Rev. John Rutledge.

The service starts at 11:30 a.m. and won't end until around 3 p.m. The road is packed hard with discarded oyster shells that islanders have laid intermittently for as long as anyone can remember. The morning sun has cleared the eastern horizon — a time described as *dayclean* by the locals.

The church is almost full when Mary and her family arrive. The Rev. Rutledge, 40, sits in a wing-back chair behind the altar. A large oak lectern is at center stage. The pastor is a big man with a full head of curly black hair. He possesses a deep baritone voice that matches his frame. He also pastors Holy Rock Baptist Church on Edisto Island. He preaches on the first and fourth Sundays at New Hope and the second and third at Holy Rock.

His sermons are long but powerful — a remarkable mix of words and song, the latter of which obviously comes from deep within his soul. He has been perfecting his delivery for more than 20 years, having grown up singing in his home church in Savannah, then schooled in the ministry in Columbia. He pastored Baptist churches in Charleston and Georgetown before moving six years ago to serve the sea island congregations.

Ushers greet Mary and her family at the door and escort them to their usual pew near the front. They squeeze into their seats tighter than usual to accommodate everyone. A small choir that sings *a cappella* fills a loft behind the altar. To the preacher's right is a small table on which rests a well-worn Bible and a large, neatly folded white towel.

As soon as Mary and the others settle in, the pastor looks to his right and nods toward the choir, which breaks out in a gospel version of "Down by the Riverside." The congregation rises, and Elder Green stands up front with his hands wrapped around a tall, padded stick, with which he pounds out the beat on the wooden floor. The stick is made of oak, its bark stripped smooth and wrapped in leather to muffle the steady thump, thump … thump, thump, thump … thump ... repeatedly as the congregants join the choir in song.

An usher passes a collection plate down one row to another usher on the other end, a process that continues until everyone has an opportunity to contribute whatever they can. The plate is placed on a table in the corner behind Mr. Green as the song ends and everyone sits down. The pastor nods toward Emma, who rises, steps to the front and turns to face the congregation:

"Dis song is to my new baby cuz'in', Miss Sarah Mary Pringle, also kno' as Kiesee, praise Gawd," she says. Emma is blessed with an angel's voice. Everyone in the sanctuary knows it because she has sung up there before. She stands tall, her hands clasped in front, takes a deep breath and begins: *"Jedus love de li'l chillum … all de li'll chillum ob de wurl'…"*

Mr. Green, stick in hand, picks up the tempo while thumping the floor, which resonates like a kettledrum. The choir members sway shoulder-to-shoulder left then right and join Emma at the chorus. *"Red an' yellow, black an' white, all dey bless in Jedus sight; Jedus love de li'll chillum ob de worl'."*

Emma finishes singing and the congregants stand and applaud. The Rev. Rutledge rises from his chair with arms outstretched and offers a prayer to all God's children on Wadmalaw, on Edisto, on the other sea islands and everywhere else on Earth as well as souls listening down from Heaven too. The ushers open the windows along each side of the building to catch a cross-breeze. The choir stands and sings the sermon hymn — "I Shall Not Be Moved."

Jedus am my Savior, I shall not be move;
In His love en' fabuh, I shall not be move,
Jis' like a tree das plant by de water,
Lawd … I shall not be move!

Meanwhile, the pastor lifts the white towel from the table and drapes it across his right shoulder. As the choir concludes the sermon song, he steps to the lectern and launches into his message entitled, "If He Can Forgive, So Should You," while occasionally lifting the cloth and drying his face. Jacob closes his eyes and listens carefully to the minister:

"De Lawd say we must forgive others who do us wrong. So hear wuh' He say. For them that don' listen to wuh Gawd say, He go look down and frown on yah … ent nobody wan' that." He pauses to dry his face. *"Listen muh brudduh and sistuh: If you don't forgive them dat do yah wrong, yah go be the one who be miserable. So let that go and moobe on. Let 'um go! Let 'um go!"* he shouts, then slams a huge right fist on the podium. *"Amen?"*

"Das right preacher," a man on the back bench stands and says as others say *"Amen."*

The choir stands and sings:
I will trus' in de Lawd;
I will trus' in de Lawd;
Sistuh will you trus' in de Lawd?
Brudduh will you trus' in de Lawd?

The service continues in this manner for hours. At 3 p.m. almost everyone in the building is soaked in sweat and near exhaustion from singing and praising and worshipping the Lord and saying amen, amen and amen. Pastor Rutledge offers the benediction and heads down the center aisle for the front door. The choir keeps on singing as its members file down the stairs from the loft and exit the building behind the pastor. The congregation follows them out the front door and into the warm sunshine. The pastor smiles broadly as he stands on the front steps, shakes each congregant's hand and thanks them for coming.

CHAPTER 17

It's evening at the Logan house. All but a single oil lamp in the front room has been extinguished. Benjamin, Charlotte and the baby are asleep in the bedroom. Anna and Mary have finished in the kitchen and sit on the porch. Mary packs her pipe, strikes a match and fires the bowl. Jacob climbs the front steps and sits on a stool between his mother and grandmother. All is quiet except for a chorus of frogs.

After a while Anna eyes Jacob and says: *"Go 'head, chil'. I kno' yah got sump'n to say, so say 'um."*

Jacob, smiles, scratches his head, and asks: *"Wuh dat preachuh talkin' 'bout t'day?"*

Mary lowers her pipe and exhales. The smoke hovers momentarily above her head before dissipating in a gentle breeze.

"He talkin' 'bout fuh'gibness," Anna tells her son. *"Kno' what dat is?"*

"Mean you ent do nutt'n back aftuh somebody do sump'n bad to yuh," Jacob responds. *"Preachuh say let dat go ... Buh Nana say hit 'um back, as long as 'e not a girl."*

"Momma," Anna turns to Mary, *"I go let you teke dis one."*

Mary smiles as she rocks back in her chair and puffs twice. *"Jacob, yah know' de story 'bout Jedus when dey nail 'um on dat cross?"*

"Yes ma'am, I 'membuh."

"Jedus tell everybody 'e fuhgib 'em, right?" Mary asks.

"Uh-huh," Jacob says.

"Das what de preachuh be talkin' 'bout," his grandmother says. *"So, if Jedus fuhgib dem people fuh doin' all dat to 'um, den us mus' fuhgib dem dat do bad ting to we. He say love yah enemy eb'n when dey hurt yah. Understan'?"*

"I tink so Nana," Jacob says. *"Buh you tell me to hit 'um back unless 'e a girl?"*

Mary rocks back and puffs twice again on her pipe. *"Hit 'um back, den furgib 'um. Wuh else on yuh mind?"*

"Well," Jacob says, *"las' night when us play hide-n-seek, I unduh de fig tree, an' I hey voices, but ent see nobody."*

"Voices unduh de fig tree?" Anna asks. *"Wuh dey say?"*

"Dey say 'He'p, he'p!' An' dat ent all. Dey grab my hand an' sta't pullin' on me."

"Den wuh happ'n, son?"

"I try to run buh I stuck. I yell but nuttin' come out. I shut muh eye tight, an' I open 'em an' I ent see nuttin' 'cept de groun' all round me. Buh I ent stuck no mo'. I get up and dat when Purvis say, 'You it!'"

"Jacob," his mother says, *"Nana done told yah don' nebuh crawl unduh de fig tree. Ent dat right?"*

"Yes ma'am."

Anna leans over and kisses Jacob on his forehead. *"Yah gotta listen when us tells yah 'bout dem ting ... OK?"*

"Yes ma'am."

"Good. Go on to bed now."

Jacob goes inside, Mary looks at Anna and whispers: *"De ol' folk say spirrut lib unduh fig tree, but I ent nebuh see one. Is you?"*

"No," Anna says, *"buh I 'membuh you tellin' me dat."*

Mary changes the subject. *"Anna, you know Miss Gladys Jenkins dat lib down de road?"*

"Yes ma'am."

"Well," Mary says, *"A long time ago, de deacon axe me to collect money fuh Pastuh Brisbane funeral, an' now a rumor go round dat I tief some a dat money an' gib it to yah daddy to help buil' dis house."*

Anna fidgets a little and scowls.

Mary continues: *"I sta't feelin' sick an' ent kno' wuh wrong until Sistuh Sally from church come to de house an' say Miss Gladys say dat I tief dat money. She say Miss Gladys mad cause de deacon axe me to collect de money, not she."* Mary pauses then adds, *"Sally say Miss Gladys pay to put a root down on me!"*

"Miss Gladys pay to put root on yah? Huh her do dat?" Anna asks.

"Well, Sally say Miss Gladys got a hank ob muh hair frum muh brush an' put 'em in a jar an' gib 'um to de root man wid de red eye, an' not long aftuh dat my head hurt so bad I can't git outta bed."

Mary leans back and rubs her forehead.

"Huh long you hab de pain?"

"Almos' a year," Mary says. *"I ent say nuttin' to nobody 'til I tell Cuz'n Pearl and Cuz'n Suzie. Pearl say, 'Mary, us go grab a shobel an' dig all de ground round de house, and dat wuh us did. Aftuh while — BIM — Pearl hit sump'n. Den — BIM — her hit 'um 'gain. Pearl reach down an' grab a jar out de dirt an' open 'um. Great Gawd! It full ob hair and de smell almos' knock we down!"*

"Momma! Wuh 'e smell like?"

"Rotten crab! Pearl throw dat jar down an' break 'um up. Susie lean obuh an' look close an' lif' up de hair, den her teke 'um inside an' throw 'um in de fiah."

"Wuh happ'n aftuh dat?"

"Well, Annie, de nex' day my head ent hurt no mo'… Ent hurt nebuh since, tank Gawd!"

Mary looked Anna in the eyes and warned, *"Dey still people on dese island dat do bad ting like dat, so watch 'em close. Dey smile big, but don' trus' 'em. When somebody grin wid all 'e teete showin', it don' alway mean 'e happy."*

Anna nods. *"I hea' yah say dat b'fo'."*

Mary nods back. *"Das de trute."*

"Momma, wuh yah do aftuh dat?"

Mary takes a deep breath. *"Yah know, fuhgib'ness ent easy. I do a lotta prayin' an' ax Gawd to gimme skrait. So I decide I gwine to Miss Gladys house an' tell her I know who pay to put de root on me … An' soon I knockin' on she door."*

"Wuh happen next?"

"Her look like her done see a ghost."

"Den wuh happ'n?"

"Well, I say good day Sistuh, see yah Sunday in church."

"Wuh her say?"

"Gladys ent crack 'e teete. Her jis look at me like she skay'd. So I tell Gladys dat I ain't mad at her, smile and go on home.

Anna shakes her head and says, *"Not me, no ma'am. I ent do dat aftuh what her did to yah."*

"Daughtuh, listen to me," Mary says. *"Not long aftuh dat Gladys pass out in church. Her hab a stroke an' ent talk right no mo'. Her can't move boff she hand an' one ob she leg. Dat wuh happ'n when yah ent do right. Her man dead, and her ent got no chillum … Dat why I teke her dinnuh an' help round she house now. Gladys ent got nobody buh me now."*

CHAPTER 18

The next morning Anna packs for her trip back to Charleston then sits out on the porch. Jacob, who is in the yard, runs up and says, *"Hey Momma, let's git some honeysuckle befo' yah go."* Mother and son walk across the yard and into the woods near the road. Their path is soon enveloped in yellow honeysuckle blooms, the vines of which run up the trees and across branches. Anna carefully selects a bloom for tasting, then Jacob does the same. Both learned early in their lives how to extract the nectar that lines the flowers' pistils.

"Dey ent tas'e like honey," Jacob says as he sucks juice from the stem.

"Dey ent spose to, Jacob. De bee use 'em to meke honey," she says.

The air is full of honeysuckle aroma as they turn and head back to the house. *"Jacob, promise me dat you ent go worry Aunt Charlotte if dem spirrut come back. She skay'd ob 'em, OK?"*

"Yes ma'am."

Anna smiles. *"An' be careful who else yah tell 'bout dem ting. Dey might smile, but dat ent mean dey ent skay'd too. You 'membuh wuh yah Nana say 'bout some folk who smile bright, showing dey teeth."*

"Yes ma'am … dat sometime dey ent happy as dey look, so watch 'em carefully."

When Jacob and his mother get back to the house they see Mr. James on his wagon out front waiting to take Leon Jr., Benjamin and Anna to the landing. Soon the bags are loaded in the wagon and everyone says their goodbyes. James and Leon Jr. climb onto the seat while Benjamin and Anna sit in the back. Charlotte and Mary wave goodbye from the porch, as Jacob walks slowly behind the wagon wishing for the day when he will be going to Charleston with his mother.

His Uncle Peter arrives not long afterward.

"Hey Momma! Sorry I late. Dey gone yet?"

"Uh-huh, an' I sad," she says as Peter wraps his arms around her. *"I got dis sack ob food fuh yah to teke back home,"* she says. *"I put dem peach leaf in dey. Don' fuhgit wuh I tell yah to do wid 'em."*

"Tank yah, Momma."

 CHAPTER 19

I t's late summer and Jacob takes a break from chopping short pieces of wood for the kitchen stove, returns to the house and asks his grandmother if she knows when Mr. James is coming for a visit.

"Why yah ax dat?"

"He wan' me to go fushin' wid 'um dis aftuhnoon."

"Uh-huh," Mary replies. *"He be hey soon, Jacob."* She had heard that James wanted Jacob to work with him on his boat.

"OK Nana," Jacob says and goes back out to the wood pile. Not long afterward James arrives.

"Hey Jacob, is yah granny in de house?"

"Yes sir!"

Mr. James walks up the steps to the door. *"Mary, yah dey? Dis James."* Jacob eases under the kitchen window and listens.

"James, I been 'spectin' you," Mary says. *"Huh yah wife been doin'?"*

"Her fine … Sho' smell good in hey. Wuh dat cookin'?"

"Yella squash wid rice an' smudduh chicken."

"Dat a Sunday dinnuh in my house," he laughs and says. *"Charlotte an' de baby OK?"*

"Uh, huh. Dey restin'."

James says, *"I tink yah know why I hey. Word trabel long an' trabel fas' round Wadmalaw. I need help in de boat an' Jacob ol' enough now…"*

"Uh huh," she says.

James smiles and says, *"Dat OK wid you!"*

"Yah ent tink him too young fuh dat?" she responds.

"Jacob ready. Big Leon would hab him out dey by now."

"Dat go gimme sump'n else to pray fuh," Mary says, *"buh dat up to you and Jacob."*

Jacob can't believe what he just overheard, and runs around to the porch.

"Jacob, yuh out dey?" Mary asks.

"Yes ma'am."

"Das wuh I thought … Come on in. Mr. James got somethin' to ax yuh."

Jacob runs up he steps and James meets him at the door.

"I talk wid yah granny an' her say yah can work wid me. I need a fust mate fuh de boat."

"Yes sir!"

"You ent go lemme down?"

"No suh, I ent go do dat."

"Alrigh', Jacob, go on now so Mr. James and me kin talk some mo'."

"Yes ma'am!"

# CHAPTER 20

It's early the next morning and Jacob is off to meet Mr. James at the landing. *"Jacob, keep yuh shirt on out dey, yah hey me?"* Mary yells as he's leaving. *"Dat sun go be hot t'day!"*

"Yes ma'am."

Jacob wastes no time getting down to the landing, where James is waiting.

"Huh yah doin' Jacob?"

"Fine."

"Alrigh', glad yah on time. Now, befo' yah come aboa'd I go gib yah some rule, so lis'en good."

"Yes sir."

"Hea' me now cause if yah ent follow muh rule, dis be de fust an' de las' time

I teke yah out wid me."

"Yes sir."

James hands Jacob a quart size tin can. *"OK. Jacob, teke dis can an' go to de stern cause you de bailer."*

Jacob grabs the can, steps onboard, turns and looks confused.

"Wuh wrong, boy? Go to de stern."

"Wuh dat?"

"Dat de back ob de boat, boy. Go back dey an' sit down," James says as he unlocks the oars and takes the middle seat. James slips past him, sits on the wide stern seat and faces forward.

"OK. I go push off now, so hold on," the captain says.

"Yes sir!"

James smiles and says, *"Turn round now and sta't bailin' when de water get back dey. De boat leak some, an' it de bailer job to scoop 'um out an' throw 'um in de creek. Dat wha' dat tin can fuh. OK?"*

"Yes sir," Jacob says as the incoming tide carries the untethered boat up the creek. James sets the oars in the locks and sits with his back to the bow. He looks at Jacob and says, *"Ent no front an' ent no back on dis boat ... You en de 'stern' and de oduh end ob de boat am de 'bow.' OK?"*

"OK," Mr. James says as he pulls back on both oars, the boat heaves forward and water collected in the bottom washes to the stern around the boy's feet. Jacob grabs the can and starts bailing.

"Dat right, Jacob, keep doin' dat til dey ent no mo'."

"Yes sir!"

When Jacob finishes bailing, he looks at James and smiles.

"Dat good, Jacob ... We goin' up de creek fuh while so stand by."

Mr. James rows steadily for a half-hour or so and Jacob sees a small tributary off the right side of the bow. James stops rowing with the oar that is in his left hand but keeps pulling with the one in his right. The boat's bow turns toward the tributary. *"We goin' 'starboard' now, an' de oduh wey be 'port.' Just 'member, left be 'port' and right be starboard; front be de 'bow' and back de 'stern.' OK?"*

He continues rowing with his right hand and holds the port oar out of the water. The boat turns past an outcrop of oysters into a narrow side creek. *"Dem shell all pile up ober dey be call a 'oystuh bank,' buh ent no money inside 'um. When de water get col' us go come back and pick up some dem oystuh, put 'em in de 'crokuh sack,' den teke 'em to de landing — dat wey de money is. We sell 'em to the man dat teke 'em to Chass'tun."*

Mr. James locks the oars, goes to the bow and grabs his cast net.

"OK, Jacob, be quiet. Us go catch some mullet. Dey ent like dem fush yah ketch under Tickle Up Bridge. Dese mullet can hey yah. So don' say nuttin'. Dey down dey listnin'."

Mr. James stands up with his cast net, puts one end of the net line around his left wrist and throws the net sidearm high and away from the boat. The lead weights around the bottom spread the net in a six-foot-wide circle, hit the water and pull the webbing down quickly to the bottom.

"Now I go pull dis rope on muh wrist, de net close up round dem fush an' trap 'em on de bottom. Den I lif' 'em an' 'e close up. Den I pull 'em up and into de boat."

Jacob leans over the starboard side and watches as James pulls in the net full of small, frantic mullet. He yanks the net into the boat, reaches down, grabs the horn (a round bone at the center) and stands as he pulls it up. The net opens and out fall the fish, which flop around in the bottom of the boat.

"Grab dem fush an' put 'em in de bucket," Mr. James yells.

Jacob scrambles forward and gets the big bucket, which he moves to the center of the boat. He uses both hands to grab each of a dozen or so slippery, three-inch-long mullets and drops them into the bucket. *"Scoop up some water and put 'um wid de fush. Dat keep 'em fresh."*

"Yes sir!"

Jacob notes how Mr. James moves effortlessly back to the center of the boat, sits down, grabs the oars and rows back into the main channel. Not long afterward Jacob sees an island on the port side.

"Dat place called Jalapa," Mr. James says. *"Nobody go obuh dey … 'e haunted."*

Jacob looks but says nothing as he stares at the island.

"Jacob," Mr. James says as he rows on past. *"Quit lookin' at dat island. Pay 'tenshun, boy, like I tell yah!"*

He rows the boat for another hour until they arrive at a huge oyster bed at the mouth of another tributary. He locks the oars, drops the anchor and lets out enough line to allow the boat to swing parallel to the shell bank.

"We go ketch a big fush now. Grab dat pole … I already rig 'um up fuh yah," James tells the boy. He points to a thick cane pole that stretches from Jacob's seat in the stern all the way to the bow.

Jacob holds the thick end of the pole while Mr. James reaches in the bucket, grabs a mullet, runs the hook at the end of the boy's line through the fish's lips. *"OK, Jacob, put 'um out dey side dat oystuh bank an' let dat mullet swim round..."*

Jacob lifts the mullet, turns his pole toward the shells, and lowers the live fish into the water. Moments later the mullet moves right, then left, then jumps up out of the water. As soon as it hits the surface — WHAM! — something grabs the bait and takes off. Jacob pulls back on the pole and sets the hook. *"I got 'um, I got 'um!"* he says as he uses both hands to hold the pole. He lifts a big bass out of the creek and drops it in the boat.

"Great Gawd, looky wuh yah got," James hollers as a big spot-tail bass flops around on the bottom of the boat.

Jacob puts down the pole and grabs the fish by the by gills with his left hand. He reaches into its mouth with his right hand and frees the hook with a quick twist.

"Dat nice ... at leas' two pound!" Mr. James says.

Jacob raises up the fish and smiles.

After the fish stops flapping, Mr. James says:

"I go talk to Mistuh Bass ... I go ax 'um if yah can come back soon an' ketch some mo'."

The solid bond between Mr. James and Jacob grew quickly as the man and boy plied their trade in the saltwater creeks in and around Wadmalaw Island. Together, they earned a little money in their seafood endeavor, and they shared what they did not sell with appreciative family members and friends. All the while Mr. James had become a loving father figure for the island boy who never knew the late Daniel Rouse.

 **CHAPTER 21**

*"*Jacob! Jacob! Wake up!"

The boy opens his eyes when he hears the man's voice, raises his head and looks around. He's been asleep on a bench inside the church, which is empty except for him and the man.

"Yuh finally wake up," the man says as he steps from the shadows. His hat is pulled down low and he's wearing a long overcoat.

"*Weh eberybody?*" Jacob asks.

"*Dey gone home and lef' yah sleepin'. I wait'n' fuh yah to wake up.*"

"*Who you is?*" asks Jacob as he sits up and rubs his eyes.

"*I jis' pass'n' through.*"

"*Wuh yah name?*"

"*Rashidi,*" the man says, "*and you is Jacob Rouse, also called Moyo Samba.*"

"*Huh yah kno' me?*"

"*I know eberybody in yah family.*"

"*Uh-huh,*" says Jacob. He can't see the man's face because the hat covers his eyes, and his collar is turned up. "*Yah kno' Mary Rouse?*"

"*Uh-huh, buh you de one I come to talk to.*" The man steps closer. Jacob eyes his shoes, which are black and shiny patten leather. Every time the stranger moves, what feels like a cool breeze stirs the room, even though the windows and doors are closed tight. The strange man sits on the bench next to the boy and says, "*Yah ent skay'd, is yah?*"

"*Uh ... I ent know yet. Huh long yuh go be hey, mistuh?*"

"*Jis a lil' while.*" The man's voice is deep and reverberant, reflective and wise.

"*Weh yuh goin'?*"

"*I on a journey, Jacob ... been trab'lin' a long time.*" The man stands up and claps his hands one time, loudly. Jacob is startled but doesn't move. He searches for a glimpse of the mysterious man's eyes.

"*Yah go be trabl'lin' too someday an' yah go meet folk 'long de wey — some good, some bad.*"

"*Uh-huh.*"

"*Jacob, I go give yah sump'n b' fo' I go.*" The man reaches into his coat pocket, pulls out a rather large black coat button and hands it to the boy. "*Dis ent jis' any ol' button. Dis special.*"

"*Un-huh.*"

"*When somebody dead an' yah at 'e funeral, stand by de casket, hol' dis up to yah eye an' look through de buttonhole. If yah see somebody sitt'n' on top de casket, dat mean de person inside hab bad spirrut hangin' ober 'um. If yah ent see nobody sittin' up dey, well, dat good.*"

Jacob, fascinated by the power of the button, smiles as he closes his fingers around the gift. "*Tank yah Mistuh Rashidi. I keep 'um wid me an' 'membuh dat.*"

They sit quietly as Jacob searches the shadow below the downturned hat for a better look at Mr. Rashidi's face. Moments later, the man turns toward the front door and says, *"Come wid me."* Jacob follows him out the front door, and without turning around, the man says, *"Go back an' meke sho' de door shut tight."*

Jacob walks back and pulls the door shut. When he turns back around, the man is gone.

"Hey Mistuh Rashidi, wait fuh me!" Jacob shouts. *"Wait ..."* That's when he tripped and fell down the front steps face down into the dirt. After a while he hears his mother calling him.

"Jacob, Jacob," Anna says softly. *"Wake up, son. You been dreamin' again."*

When he opened his eyes this time he is sitting on the front porch of Mary's house alongside his mother, who had come the previous day to Wadmalaw for a visit. *"What were you dreamin' 'bout, son?"*

Jacob rubs his eyes, looks at his mother and sits up straight in his grandmother's rocking chair. He rubs his eyes some more and says:

"I dream I in de church sleepin' on a bench and dis man wake me up. I look round an' ent nobody else dey 'cept me and dat man, who say 'e name Rashidi. Him hab a wide brim hat down low obuh 'e eye, an' hab a long coat, an' shiny black shoe, an' say 'e kno' me an' you an' muh daddy. An' 'e say 'e been trab'lin' long time. An' 'e gib me a special button. An' 'e ax if I want to see wuh he got outside. So us go outside an' 'e say go back an' shut de door, meke sho' it tight. Aftuh I do dat I turn round an' 'e gone. Dat when I trip an' fall down the front step, an' you wake me up and hey we is."

Anna closes her eyes and doesn't say anything for almost a full minute. Then she looks directly into her son's eyes and says, *"Dat man yah gran' daddy, Big Leon, who also name Rashidi. Did 'e ax you to go wid him?"*

Jacob saw that she was worried. *"No ma'am. Him gimme de button an' say us gwine outside to see sump'in' an' I wake up. Huccome him ent lemme see 'e face?"* he says as he checks his pockets for the button but can't find it.

Anna says patiently: *"Jacob, promise me dat if yah gran' daddy come round 'gain an' ax yuh to go wid him, tell him no. Unduhstan'?"*

"Yes ma'am."

CHAPTER 22

J acob didn't think much about meeting his long-dead grandfather. But there certainly wasn't anything natural about this encounter . The following week he returned to the church and searched the dirt near the front steps until he found the big black button. He picked it up, cleaned it with his shirt tail, slipped it in his pocket and went back to the house. That night he put the button into a small box he kept under his mattress and went to sleep. Later he heard someone, opened his eyes and there stood Big Leon wearing the wide-brim hat, the overcoat with the collar turned up and his black shoes.

"Dat you Granddaddy?"

"Uh-huh, dis me ... I hey to tell yah 'bout how yah gwine be trab'lin' like me."

"Whycome?" the boy asks.

"Cause yah special."

"I go be trab'lin' wid you?"

"No, Jacob, not wid me. When yuh journey start, mine end."

Jacob remembered his mother's warning, so he asked, *"Granddaddy, do Gawd kno' 'bout dis?"*

"Oh yeah, He kno', buh das all I go say 'bout dat now."

Jacob tried to get up but couldn't move, like when he was under the fig tree. The curtains blew out the bedroom window and he woke up.

A month or so later Jacob was sitting on the porch in the rocking chair. He closed his eyes and nodded off. This time he dreamed he was walking down a narrow dirt road and heard Big Leon say, *"Hol' up, Jacob, hol' up ... I got another ting fuh yuh."* The old man stepped out from behind a tree, walked past the boy to a nearby evergreen bush about four feet tall with red berries. He reached in his pocket, pulled out a small knife, cut off an odd wrinkled twig, removed its leaves and handed it to Jacob.

"Wuh dis is?" the boy asked.

"Dis' de debil backbone'. Put 'um in yah pocket an' don' tell nobody. Hea' wuh I sayin'?"

"Yes sir."

His grandfather said the six-inch-long stem possessed healing powers, but only special people could use it properly. *"I go sho' yah mo' plant an' root an' ting dat fuh he'pin' folk 'long de way,"* he said, adding, *"Gawd go work wid yah, Moyo Samba, so be ready, OK?"*

CHAPTER 23

It's late afternoon on Wadmalaw. Mary, Anna and Charlotte are preparing to go to the late Miss Gladys Jenkins' wake at the praise house, a smaller one-room building than the church and not as far away. Anna has come from Charleston to pay her respects for Mary's recently departed neighbor.

"Nana," Charlotte says. *"Dey say Miss Gladys bin one ob dem nasty hag. Dat right?"*

"No," Mary says, adding, *"Gladys' sistuh be de hag."*

"Miss Ruth?" Charlotte asks.

"Uh-huh."

Emma and Jacob, who are on the porch, overhear the conversation.

"I 'membuh Daddy say Miss Ruth a hag, buh I ent pay 'um no mind," Emma whispers to Jacob. *"Her been dead fuh while."* They keep listening.

"Well," says Mary, *"I ent teke no chance wid Miss Ruth. Her stop by an' ax fuh cup a rice. I tell 'um I ent got no rice … buh dat a lie, an' I ax de Lawd fuhgibness fuh dat. Fac' is, if yah gib sump'n out yah house to a hag, her gwine slip back in at night, teke she skin off, hang 'um on de door, jump on yah and try to teke yah breat' away. Dat wuh de ol' folk say … Ent nobody wan' no nasty hag to ride yah like dat. Yah gotta thro' salt on 'um to get 'um off. Salt burn 'um up cause hag ent got no skin on 'um."*

Anna says, *"Uh-huh, uh-huh. Daddy tell me don' laugh round Miss Ruth cause if her can count yah teete, her comin' back dat night an' ride yah … When Miss Ruth come round, I put muh hand obuh muh mout."*

"'Nuf talk 'bout nasty old hag en all dat," Mary says, raising her voice: *"Yuh know dem big ear out dey on dat porch."*

Jacob and Emma look at each other and smile.

Moments later, Anna whispers, *"Hey Momma … Jacob say 'e dream 'bout Daddy."*

Charlotte says, *"I ent wanna hea' no mo' 'bout dat. I gittin' out dis room right now… I ent wanna kno' nuttin' 'bout dat."*

Emma and Jacob hear Charlotte say she is leaving, so they move closer to the front door and listen some more …

"Jacob dream Daddy come to see 'um," Anna says.

"Well, I ent su'prise. Jacob special," his grandmother says.

"Jacob say he sleepin' alone in de church an' somebody say, 'Wake up!' Jacob open 'e eye an' see a man in dey wid him."

"Wuh else?" Mary asks.

"Jacob ax, 'Who dat?' … an' de man say 'e name Rashidi."

"Dat yah Daddy spirrut name," Mary says. *"Wuh else?"*

"Jacob ent see de man face 'cause de man hat pull down low … Buh 'e reach in 'e coat pocket an' gib Jacob a big, black button."

"Lawd, Lawd!" Mary sighs. *"Yah kno' wuh Jacob able to do wid dat button?"*

"I sho' do!" Anna says.

"Did Rashidi ax Jacob to go wid him?"

"I ax Jacob dat, an' 'e say no."

"OK," Mary says, adding that, at Big Leon's funeral, Jacob — who was just a baby — was passed over the casket by his uncles to help keep the child safe for the rest of his life. *"So … I ent spose to worry 'bout dat."* She stands, raises her voice and tells Jacob and Emma it's time to get dressed for Miss Gladys' wake.

Later that day, Mary and her family arrive at the praise house. Some folks are already inside an a few men stand around a fire they built in the yard. Smoke from the blaze keeps gnats and mosquitoes away.

"Good eben'n' eberybody," Mary says as she enters the building.

The praise house is small; it can accommodate only fifteen people at the most. It's where members of the church gather informally to meet, socialize, share food, sing, dance, celebrate and attend wakes. The casket is up front and folks are seated on benches along the walls. Two tables are positioned longways down the middle of the room for food. Oil lanterns burn bright inside the old wooden building, which only has two windows, one on each side of the entrance, and a cedar shingled roof.

Mary and her entourage approach the casket to pay respects to Miss Gladys. The coffin is open and thin netting covers Miss Gladys' face. As Jacob waits in line, he pulls the big button from a pocket, closes one eye and looks with the other through the hole at the coffin. He is startled when he feels a touch on his shoulder.

"Dat enough of dat," Anna, who stands behind him, whispers sternly in his ear. He slips the button back into his pocket, turns, walks out front and joins the men around the fire.

Several hours pass and dozens of islanders have stopped in to pay their respects. The funeral and burial will be the next day at the church. Mary and her family arrive back at the house at 9 p.m. and go to bed. The next day, on their way to the church, Charlotte, Anna and Emma take turns carrying little Sarah. As they arrive, several men are lifting the casket off a horse-drawn wagon and carry it inside the sanctuary. Mary and the others fall in behind the pallbearers. As they enter the building the choir burst into song:

Swing low, sweet chariot,
Com'n' fuh to caya' me home,
Swing low, sweet chariot,
Com'n' fuh to caya' me home.

The song ends, the pallbearers carry in the casket and place it on a small table in front of the altar. Miss Edwards, the choir director, turns around and says, *"Tank all of yah fuh comin' to dis 'home-going' ceremony fuh Sistuh Gladys Jenkins."* The Rev. Brownlee sits silently in the pastor's chair and waits for family members and close friends to be seated up front. After everyone is settled, he stands and lifts his arms like he's trying wrap them around everyone in the room.

"We are all Miss Gladys' family today. Each of us is her brudduh or sistuh now, an' I sho' Gladys 'preciate dat. Each of us am brudduh an' sistuh in Jedus Christ too… Dat mean we got job to do," he says as he looks down on the coffin, *"cause nobody kno' when dey goin' home to be wid Gawd Almighty — just like Sistuh Gladys."*

"Amen," someone shouts.

Jacob, who is sitting in the second row, again grabs the button and narrows his focus through the tiny hole. His heart races … but he sees nothing unusual.

Pastor Brownlee holds forth to his flock for almost an hour before shouting, *"Gawd is Good!"* Several congregants yell *"Amen,"* and another says, *"Dat right … Praise Jedus!"*

The pastor says:

"Sistuh Gladys spirrut on a journey home now, buh her body ent. Her spirrut nebuh die, uh huh. De Lawd call Sistuh Gladys an' she tra'blin' to her heabenly

home right now. Amen?"

The congregants say in unison, *"Amen,"* and the choir stands up and sings:
Some glad mornin' when dis' life be obuh,
I'll fly away
To muh home on Gawd c'lestial sho'e,
I'll fly away!

Everybody in the church sings and moves with the beat, which is accented by the man up front in a corner, holding a big stick with both hands and thumping it in rhythm on the wooden floor. The pallbearers step forward, lift the coffin, carry it out the front door and down the steps as everyone follows to the open grave out back. They gather around the coffin as the pastor reads Bible passages before concluding with the verse about people being born of dust and returning to dust, and the benediction. Everyone leaves except for the pallbearers, who remove their jackets, roll up their sleeves and use ropes to lower the coffin into the ground. They take turns shoveling dirt until the grave is covered. Folks will return later and leave flowers and mementoes that honor Gladys' life.

Jacob and his family return home without saying a word.

 # CHAPTER 24

I t's the second week of January 1917 and the front room fire burns brightly in Mary Logan's house on Wadmalaw Island. She calls for Jacob, who is on the porch:

"Come yah, boy!"

"Yes ma'am."

"Git some mo' wood, den go in de shed an' bring mo' moss fuh dese crack en de flo' to keep de col' out."

"Yes ma'am."

"An' put yah coat an' hat on."

"Alrigh' Nana."

Jacob cut enough wood to last for weeks and stored enough moss in the shed to fill all the cracks in the floors and around the windows too. But Charlotte has not been feeling well for three days. Mary gives her a teaspoon of castor oil daily and rubs her chest with mutton suet as a precautionary measure. Jacob returns to the house with an arm full of wood.

"*Put some in de fiah place an' some short piece by de stobe. I go start cookin' soon,*" Mary says.

"*Yes ma'am,*" he says and heads back out to the shed. When he returns, he says, "*Nana, a cat out by de shed. Kin I gib' 'um some food?*"

"*I done tell you I ent want no cat. Feed 'um an' 'e go stay an' yah ent go get rid of 'um. Yah great-grandmomma tell me 'bout a cat dey hab in de house. She come home one day an' she sistuh sick in de bed, an' de cat on de bed stand'n' obuh she head. Yah great-grandmomma grab de broom an' hit de cat, an' dat ting jump out de winduh. Dat when her sistuh say she can't breathe 'cause de cat suck de air out she mout'. Some folk say cat be good luck, but I ent tink so — not fuh dis family.*" Mary looks directly at Jacob: "*A cat also got de power to run tru' a room an' meke de whole place shake.*"

Charlotte listens quietly from the bedroom. She has heard this story before.

Mary continues, "*Jacob, go back out dey an' chase dat ting away. Yah hey me?*"

"*Yes ma'am.*" Jacob decides it would be best if he didn't tell her he had been playing with the cat for several days. He had given the cat some fish heads too.

"*OK, Charlotte,*" Mary says as she steps into the bedroom. "*Sip dis broth. Careful, now, 'e hot!*"

Charlotte holds the bowl to her nose and says, "*Dis smell good, wuh all in um?*"

"*Lemme see, onion an' celery, an got chicken neck in dey too,*" Mary says. "*Teke yah time now. Dat he'p git yah bettuh. I go check on de baby.*"

Mary walks over to the child and looks at Sarah's face. She is almost a year old now. Her complexion is darker now, more like Charlotte's.

"*Momma, de chicken neck taste good. I feel a lot bettuh already,*" Charlotte says.

"*OK teke 'um slow … Dis ebnin' us go hab cootuh stew. I sta't mekin' 'um las' night in de big pot. Den I put 'um in de fiahplace and let 'um slo' cook.*"

"*I ent membuh nutt'n 'bout no cootuh,*" Charlotte says.

"*Uh huh. Peter bring dat big turtle hey de oduh day. You ent 'membuh?*"

"*No Momma.*"

Jacob comes back inside with some moss in hand.

"*Boy, wuh yah been doin' out dey all dat time?*" Mary asks.

"*I chase dat cat off buh 'e come back, so I chase 'um off agin.*"

"*Dat ting gone now?*" Mary asks.

"Yes ma'am."

"OK."

Jacob puts down the moss and warms his hands at the fireplace. He stares past the cook pot into the embers as his fingers thaw.

"Jacob. Jacob," Mary says. *"Yah look'n in dat fiah like yah go jump in."*

"Sorry, Nana."

Jacob was thinking about the cat, and as he looks into the fire he sees its eyes, and the more the boy looks, the more he sees of the cat's face staring back. He is mesmerized.

"Is yah sho' dat cat gone?" Mary asks.

"Uh, I tink so," Jacob says.

"Go back out dey an' meke sho'."

"Yes ma'am."

After a while Jacob returns to the house and goes into the bedroom

"Morn'n' Auntie. Feel'n' bettuh?"

Charlotte, who is sitting up in the bed and combing her hair says, *"Uh-huh."*

Jacob stuffs moss in cracks in the floor and around the window. The walls are covered with newspapers for insulation.

"Yah kno' wuh yuh doin'?" Charlotte asks with a smile.

"Uh huh, dis wuh de man ob de house 'pose to do," he replies.

"Boy, you ent no man ob de house; yah jis' a goober head," Charlotte says with a laugh. *"When I git all de wey feel'n' bettuh, I go cut yah back side. Den I go see huh much man yuh is."*

"Auntie, quit jokin' wid me."

"OK, Spooky, go on, git out dis room," she says, laughing.

Jacob steps into the main room and Mary asks, *"Yah 'pose to be putt'n' moss down? All I hea' back dey is laugh'n."*

"Yes ma'am, I already put moss in all dem crack cause I de man ob de house."

"Who say yuh is?" she asks with a smirk.

"Das wuh Uncle Leon an' Uncle Peter tell me. Dey say I gotta look aftuh ya'll."

"Alrigh', Mistuh Big Man Jacob, put moss down in de res' ob de house," Mary says. *"When yah through wid dat, watch Sarah while I he'p Charlotte wid she hair."*

"Yes ma'am."

Mary tells Charlotte to sit by the kitchen stove, which is already fired up. *"I go teke yah hair an' plat 'em down two side. OK?"*

"OK," Charlotte replies.

An hour later, Mary and Charlotte, with her hair plaited, move over by the fireplace.

"Ent be long b' fo' you, Benjamin an' Sarah go move to Bewfu't," Mary says. *"Benjamin go like workin' in de lumbuh-ya'd down dey. Bewfu't ent big like Chaa'stun."*

"Uh huh," Charlotte replies.

"I glad Benjamin ent go be workin' en Chass'tun on de water no mo'," Mary says. *"I pray fuh him an' Leon Jr. when dey dey. Big Leon lost two cuz'n' out dey."*

"Uh-huh. I be tink'n 'bout dat too. Dat lumbuh-ya'd safe en de pay bettuh too," Charlotte says.

"I go miss yah," Mary says.

"Momma, is yuh alrigh'?"

"Uh-huh, jis tink'n' dat lil' Sarah be sump'n else. Her 'mind me ob muh momma."

"When us git settle down dey, I go meke fruit pusurbe an' sell em in de market," Charlotte says. *"Den I go get a job as a hotel chef."*

"Das good."

"Uh huh."

"Yah kin mek a lil' money, an' he'p Benjamin too."

"Yes ma'am. Das de plan"

"I pray fuh dat," Mary says.

That afternoon Mary asks Jacob to take some turtle stew to Miss Ella, who helps at the island school. She hadn't been to church in several months. *"I tink she sick. Teke dis en leebe em wid who down dey wid she."*

"Alrigh' Nana," he says. *"I go stop an' see Arthur on de wey back, OK?"*

"OK, but don' stay long."

"Yes ma'am."

"Hey Charlotte, 'membuh I told you Peter bin by an' bring dat cootuh?" Mary asks.

"Yes ma'am, I 'membuh."

"Well, dat when I talk wid Peter 'bout Mamie."

"You hab 'pose to gib him sometin' to teke back to help Mamie," Charlotte says.

"Uh-huh. I gib Peter peach tree leebe, an' him say, 'Momma, aftuh I rub dem leebe on Mamie leg an' chest an' put a pan of water unduh de bed, de nex' day her ent got febuh no mo'. I tell Mamie her got a root on her or maybe de house

got bad spirrut up in dey. I say …"

Charlotte interrupts Mary before she finishes her sentence. *"Momma, you say bad spirrut in dat house. Huh yuh know dat?"*

"I ent kno' fuh sho', buh de ol' folk say de house ent nebuh been bless. Dat ent good. When somebody dead in a unbless house an' nobody cover de mirror in de room, de bad spirrut still in dey try'n' to git out. Uh-huh, uh-huh, das wuh de old folk say."

"Wuh happ'n nex'?"

"All kind ob ting," Mary says. *"Bad spirrut meke de man an' de ooman argue all de time, an' meke de chillum rude, an' meke people in de house sick. Ent no peace in dey aftuh dat."*

"Huh yah git 'um out?"

"Well, a preachuh can bless de house. Him go in all de room an' pray. Dat do sometime. Buh spirrut tricky. You kin bless de house all yah want, buh dem bad spirrut go stay right in dey."

"Momma, I ent nebuh hea' nutt'n like dat b'fo'."

"Oh yeah. De oduh ting yah kin do is git sky blue paint an' put 'um round de door an' all de winduh frame. Den yuh git cinnamon and sprinkle inside all de room, and all de corner too. Ent no bad spirrut go like dat," Mary says.

"Huccome de paint be blue like de sky?"

"Dat de color ob heaben, an' dat also wey de Lawd lib. Dem bad spirrut skay'd ob Gawd, an' sky blue 'bout peace an' Heaben … Das de trute."

"So huccome us ent paint yah window an' door sky blue?" Charlotte asks.

"Cause yah daddy buil' dis house from de ground up, an' de preachuh done bless ebery room, ebery wall, ebery corner, ebery door an' ebery window an' de chimney too. Dat why ent no bad sprirrut in hey!"

Charlotte rubs her chin. *"OK, den huccome spooky Jacob see spirrut in dis house?"*

Mary slaps her hand on a knee. *"Ha! I kno' dat wuh yah fix'n to ax. Listen to me good: Jacob see spirrut in dis house but dat one ent bad. Jacob see yah daddy round hey. Das all. Ent been no bad spirrut hey."*

⬤ CHAPTER 25

Jacob arrives at Miss Ella's house and knocks twice on the door. An old woman opens it slowly. It's dark inside. After a long pause, a woman asks, *"Well, hello Sugah! Huh you is?"* Jacob recognizes Miss Bessie Jones' voice from church. She calls all children Sugar.

"Morn'n' Miss Bessie."

She smiles, says Jacob has grown a lot, and asks, *"Huh Sistuh Mary an' de fambly do?"*

"Dey all good," Jacob says. *"Nana ax me to bring dis food to Miss Ella."*

Miss Bessie takes the package and smiles. *"Ummm, dis smell good. Yah Nana always do fuh oduh folk. Gawd bless she fuh dat. Come on in."*

"Yes ma'am."

A stench fills the front room. Smells like old people, Jacob decides. There's a fire in the fireplace but it's not warm inside. He sees plenty of wood near the hearth, more than enough to last through the night.

"I gotta go on now. Nana need me back at de house," he says.

"Alrigh' Sugah. Tell yah Nana dat Ella say tank yah."

"Yes ma'am."

On the way home, Jacob stops at Arthur's house. They haven't seen each other for two weeks because the island's sole teacher has been out with the flu. The boys have become closer friends since Emma left for Savannah to attend the boarding school.

Emma was the smartest student in her class on Wadmalaw Island, and the teacher often gave her books to read at home. The teacher stayed on the island one Saturday morning, met Emma inside the schoolhouse and asked her to take an achievement test. A lady from Savannah was there who ran a school for gifted girls who want to become teachers. After they graded Emma's test they asked to meet with her aunt, who lived within walking distance of the school.

The teacher told the aunt that Emma had scored high on the test and that she could go to the special school in Savannah free of tuition, room and board. The lady from Savannah smiled broadly and said Emma would room with three other smart girls, and in addition to being trained to become teachers, they would study home economics, cooking and tailoring.

 CHAPTER 26

Mary gets up from her chair and goes to the stove to get a cup of hot tea. She feels sharp pains in her hands and knees … *"A sho' sign of rain,"* she whispers to herself, *"an' de mo' 'e hurt de bigguh de sto'm."*

"Hab'n trouble wid yuh knee?" Charlotte asks.

"Uh-huh.

"Bad weadhuh com'n'?" Charlotte asks.

"Ent kno'. Might jis be Ol' Cuz'n Arthur payin' me a visit."

"Ol' Cuz'n Arthur? Who dat?"

"Ha! Cuz'n Arthur Wrightus," Mary says. *"He ent come round to see yah yet 'cause yah ent old enough. Dat why dey call 'um "Ol' Cuz'in. He visit old folk so much 'e like a 'membuh ob de fambly. Buh nobody wan' him fuh sho'. Das why I got a coppuh bracelet round muh ankle and one on muh wrist too. Ol' Cuz'n Arthur ent like dat."*

"Huh, I kno' yah kiddin',' Charlotte smiles and says. *"How long you hab dem bracelet?"*

"B'fo' you born," Mary says. *"Dese yah Granny bracelet. When her pass, I got 'em. I go leeb' 'em fuh you when I go. Dey pull de ache out yah bone, tank Gawd."*

"Tank yah Momma," Charlotte says, then asks: *Wuh happen aftuh Peter paint 'e house trim sky blue?"*

"Well, Peter say Mamie sta't feelin' bettuh, an' aftuh while dey be laughin' an' carryin' on like dey spose to. Dey go back to church too. Dat wuh happen when dem bad spirrut gone, tank Gawd."

"Das good," Charlotte says.

"Uuh-huh. I ent see yah brudduh look dat happy since 'e marry Mamie."

"Momma, when me an' Benny git our place, I tell 'um to buy a bucket ob sky blue paint an' put 'um round de door an' winduh."

Mary smiles and both women burst into laughter.

Jacob arrives, removes his hat and coat, and heads to the fireplace to warm his hands. *"Hello, Auntie. Hello, Nana,"* he says. *"It cold outside."*

Charlotte says, *"Since you be a man now an' all, why ent yah getting' warm at yah gal house?"*

"I ent got no gal," Jacob says.

"Who at de house wid Sistuh Ella?" Mary asks.

"Miss Bessie be dey. Her say Miss Ella in de bed. Miss Bessie say tank yuh fuh de food ... Nana, kin I hab some co'nbread?"

"Yuh sho' can ... I gib yah a big piece an' some hot tea too."

"OK Nana... Wan' me to cut 'um?"

"Lawd no!" Mary laughs and says. *"You got de heaby hand ... Ent be nuttin lef' fuh us when yah through."*

⚫ CHAPTER 27

It's a Saturday afternoon in early February. Mary has gone to check on Miss Ella, and Jacob and his Aunt Charlotte are in the main room when they hear someone on the porch. *"Hey Spooky, you go let me in?"*

Jacob goes to the door and Emma pushes past him. *"Hello Cuz'n Charlotte,"* she says.

"Great Gawd, girl, de ol'uh' yah git, de mo' yah look like yah grand-momma," Charlotte says. *"Yah purty as ebuh."*

Emma smiles and adjusts her dark blue beret. *"School close; dat big storm las' week blow de roof off de place."*

Jacob admires Emma's gray tweed overcoat and hat embossed with a golden eagle. He eyes her shiny black shoes and neat blue-and-gray plaid skirt, which reaches her ankles. Her unbraided hair is pulled back and she appears to have grown an inch or two.

"Wey Nana at?" she asks Charlotte.

"Down to Miss Ella house. Momma go be su'prise to see yah, and lookin' like a lady!"

"Thank yuh," Emma says and turns to Jacob. *"Wuh wrong wid you ... Cat got yah tongue?"*

"I kin talk ... I talk'n' right now."

"Wey Sarah?"

"Obuh dey in she bed," Charlotte says.

Emma walks over to the baby and smiles. *"Her look like Cuz'n Benny."*

"Das wuh eberybody say," Charlotte says as she puts on her coat and heads for the door. *"I ent be gone long. If her wake up, gib she her bottle."*

"Alrigh' Auntie," Jacob says.

Charlotte leaves and Jacob looks at Emma, who says, *"Spooky, why is yah starin' at me like dat?"*

"Jis look'n'."

Emma removes her hat and coat and puts them on the table.

"Wuh dat bird on yah hat?" Jacob asks.

"Das a eagle. My school call Beasley School fuh Colored Girls… We de Eagles. Das our mascot."

"Das yuh wuh?"

"Our mascot … de animal we spose to act like. Eagle fly high in de sky. Dat wuh dey wan' us to do too."

"People ent know huh to fly," he says, frowning.

"I ent mean fuh real."

"Uh-huh," Jacob says as he eyes Emma's hair. It's the first time he has seen her without braids. *"Yuh like dat school?"*

"At fust, I skay'd 'bout livin' dey, but not no more."

"Wuh yuh learn dey?"

"Lotta ting, Jacob: Math, readin', writin', English, jography, sewin', cookin' an' etiquette too."

"Eti-wuh?"

"Etiquette … good manners."

"Uh-huh. Dey got any boy at dat school?"

"It a girl school, Jacob, ent no boy dey. I stay in wuh call a 'dormitory' wid two girl wid me in my room: Jeannie an' Doris. Us each hab a bed, an' de room hab a big glass winduh."

"Who dem girl?"

"Jeannie from Sapelo, Georgia, an' Doris down to Daufuskie. Both of dem place be island like Wadmalaw."

"Huh long yah go be at dat school?"

"Lemme see … Af'uh dis year, I got t'ree mo'… den I go be a school teacher."

"You! A teachuh?" he smirks.

"Yes!"

Jacob's smirk disappears. *"Yah ent go lib on Wadmalaw no mo'?"*

"No, buh I go visit a lot."

Jacob, obviously shaken, turns and sits on the couch. Emma sits next to him. They say nothing.

Moments later, Mary returns.

"Hello Nana!" Emma stands and says, smiling broadly.

"Great Gawd! Is you Emma Jane Rouse right hey in muh house?" Mary says and hugs Emma. *"Girl, yah grow'd up ... lookin' mo' like a Rouse now wid yah fancy cap an' dat dress an' dem shiny shoe like yuh gwine to church."*

"Dis wuh all de girl wear at muh school."

"Uh-huh. Turn round, girl, lemme see." Emma slowly turns all the way around. *"Dat bootiful, girl."*

Emma lifts her skirt slightly so Mary can see her socks. Jacob has never seen Emma wearing laced-up shoes and white socks.

"Great Gawd," he says.

Emma smiles. Jacob sits back and stares at the ceiling.

"Huh long yah go be hey baby?" Mary asks.

"I go back Sunday."

"Dat nice! Y'all wan' a lil' sump'n to eat?"

"Yes ma'am!" Jacob and Emma reply in unison.

"Well, I got two sweet 'tater in de fiah," Mary says as she grabs a long, iron fork next to the fireplace. She stirs the coals a little then pokes two large sweet potatoes.

"Uh-huh, dey ready. I teke 'em to de table fuh yah."

"I miss yuh cookin' Nana," Emma says as she sits down, *"speshly yah pound cake. Can yah make some fuh me to teke back to school."*

"Sho', chil'. I glad to do dat."

"Nana, yah ent go gib' dat sick'nen girl all de cake, is yah?" Jacob chimes in.

"Wuh wrong wid yah, boy? Emma ent sick'nen. Her purty!"

Emma sticks out her tongue at Jacob, who finally manages a smile, stands and joins her at the table.

 # CHAPTER 28

It's late afternoon on Wadmalaw. Mary, Charlotte, Emma and Jacob sit near the fireplace and talk about the future.

"Emma," Charlotte says, *"Sarah, Benny and me go moobe to Bewfu't soon."*

"Ya'll ent gwine to Chass'tun?" Emma asks.

"Not no mo'," Charlotte says. *"Benny go work in de lumbuh-ya'd down dey.*

Him ent go be on dem dock no mo', an' I glad."

Jacob has heard all this before and doesn't like it. He stands, grabs his hat and coat and walks out on the porch. Emma puts on her beret and follows.

"Wuh wrong, Jacob?"

He doesn't answer.

"Jacob, wuh wrong?"

"Nuttin' wrong."

"You ent fool me! Somethin' wrong. Why you walk out like dat?"

Jacob looks down. *"Nuttin'."*

She puts her hands on her hips. *"Jacob Moyo Samba Rouse, I know dat ent right. Wuh wrong?"*

Jacob steps into the yard and stares at his shoes. *"You at school in Savannah; Auntie an' all dem gwine to Bewfu't … Jis me an' Nana go be lef'."*

"I be back frum time to time," she says.

A chilly wind off the Atlantic rattles the oak tree's massive limbs as leaves swirl round the yard. Emma elbows Jacob. He manages a smile, they go back inside and sit with the others. Mary lights her pipe, takes two puffs and says, *"Emma, huh ol' yah is?"*

"I be 14 in three mont."

"An' Jacob, huh ol' is you?"

"I be 13 in December."

"Uh-huh," Mary says. *Jacob say him be a man now, an' Emma go be a teachuh. Now a good time to talk 'bout de future … Ya'll learnin' dat dis worl' hab lotta up an' down. Uh huh. I be gwine home to de Lawd someday, so 'membuh wuh I say when I say dis: Ebery tub gotta stan' on 'e own bottom."*

Jacob and Emma say nothing while Mary takes two more puffs from her pipe. *"Y'all ent chillum no mo'—yah 'bout to go out in de worl', an' when yah out dey, yah mus' be ready fuh all kind'uh ting. Dey go be good day an' bad day too an' some ob both dem ting in de same day. So 'membuh to keep de Lawd in front yuh all de time… an' don' be shy 'bout prayin'. Hey wuh I say? An' don' fuget to help oduh folk when dey need help. Stan' in de gap fuh 'em till de Lawd step in. Got dat?"*

"Yes ma'am," they say in unison.

"Dat all I go say fuh now. Now gib Nana a hug," which they did.

⬤ CHAPTER 29

It's the day before Emma goes back to school. She and Jacob take a short-cut to her house, about a mile away. Jacob stops and whispers, *"A big buck obuh dey. See 'um?"*

She stops, turns and looks into the woods. *"I ent see nut'n'."*

He pulls her closer to him and points to two tall pines. *"See, right in dey."*

"Oh, I see 'um now," she whispers. *"He big."*

"Uh huh. If I hab a shotgun, I drop 'um. Uncle Peter say 'e teach me to shoot 'e gun, buh Nana say 'No!'. Her skay'd sump'n bad might happ'n like wuh happ'n to Big Leon. Buh Uncle Peter say he be only ten yea' ol' when 'e shoot 'e fust rabbit, and now I is fo'teen."

"Nana skay'd 'cause her love you," Emma whispers.

"But I wanna hunt fuh rabbit an' coon, an' possum, an' dat big buck obuh dey. Dat wuh de man ob de house 'spose to do."

Smiling, Emma whispers, *"You de man ob Mary house?"*

"Uh-huh."

Emma steps back on a dead branch, which cracks, and off bounds the deer into the deep woods. *"Sorry 'bout dat, Jacob."*

Jacob and Emma continue walking.

"My momma com'n' nex' mont'," Jacob says. *"I sho' be glad when her do. She go be hey fuh week. Das wuh Mr. Sammy tell Nana."*

"I ent go see her," Emma says. *"I ent be back to Wadmalaw 'til Memorial Day."*

"OK," Jacob says. *"I see yuh on Memorial Day. Us hab a good time las' year, init?"*

"Un-huh. Lotta folk go be hey fuh dat," she says.

"Uh-huh."

As they approach Emma's house they stop and look at each other in silence. *"Well, dis when us part way,"* she says.

"U-huh."

Emma rubs his shoulder, looks directly into his eyes and says, *"Teke care of yahself, an' teke care a dem 'oomens cause yah de man ob de house now."*

"OK," Jacob says and again stares at the ground. *"I go tell eberybody on Wadmalaw dat Cuz'n Emma gwine be a teachuh."*

CHAPTER 30

I t's been a week since Emma returned to school. Jacob, Mary and Charlotte are sitting in the main room when he says, *"I wanna tell yah 'bout a dream."*
Both women sit up straight.

"I ent wanna hey nutt'n' 'bout no dead people!" Charlotte declares.

"No Auntie, muh dream 'bout fush."

"Oh, OK, go 'head."

Mary laughs, *"Gal, why is yah skay'd 'bout dem ting?"*

"Momma, I ent kno'. Jis is."

Jacob knows they would be shocked if he told them about the conversations he's been having with his grandfather lately, but keeps that to himself.

"Tell us 'bout yah fush dream," Charlotte says.

"OK. Dis dream bin two mont ago 'bout me, Mr. James, Mr. Sammy, Arthur an' Purvis. Us at de land'n' an' I ketch a big fush. Buh ent nobody kno' wuh kind 'e be. So I bring 'um back to de house an' wash 'um off at de pump. Den I try to clean de scale off, buh nuttin' come off. Well, I bring 'um in de house an' ax Nana fuh help … She scrape and scrape dat fush but ent no scale on 'um."

"Wuh happ'n den?" asks Charlotte.

"Nana ax, 'Wuh kind'uh fush dis be dat ent go no scale? Teke dat ting an' chunk 'um in de woods!' … Dat when I wake up," Jacob says.

"Momma, ent you say if yuh dream 'bout fush somebody in de family go hab a baby?" Charlotte asks.

"Gal, yuh teke de word out muh mout'! Dream 'bout fush wid scale, baby go be a girl; dream 'bout fush widout no scale, baby go be a boy. Uh-huh."

"Ent me go hab anudduh baby," Charlotte vows, laughing.

"No, buh yuh got two brudduh an' a sistuh too. Could be one of dem; could be somebody else in de fambly, uh-huh. Us go soon find out …"

Jacob doesn't want to hear anything more about fish and babies. *"Nana, I go rake' de ya'd."*

"Alrigh'. Feed dem chicken fuh me," Mary says.

"Yes ma'am."

As soon as the door slams shut, Mary turns to Charlotte: *"Jacob gotta burden … 'e kno' wuh go happ'n b'fo' 'e happ'n."*

"I tink yah right, Momma. Sometime Jacob in 'nudduh worl' all by heself wid dat strange look on 'e face, an' ent tell nobody why."

"Dat right, Charlotte. De ol'uh Jacob git, de skronger dat burden go be."

"Un-huh. I joke wid 'em 'bout see'n' ting an' all, buh wuh hap'nin' to Jacob be real," Charlotte says nervously.

"Amen! Keep axe'n' de Lawd to meke dat boy skrong," Mary replies.

As Jacob rakes sweeping waves in the dirt out front, he thinks about his mother coming to visit before Charlotte, Benny and Sarah leave for Beaufort. It's been months since he last saw her, and hopes she'll tell him when they will live together in Charleston. He also wonders how far it is from Charleston to Savannah because someday he wants to visit Emma in Savannah.

 # CHAPTER 31

A nna is the only person working in the tailor's shop on King Street in Charleston. Mr. Broadnax, the owner, left earlier for the bank as usual. Broadnax Tailoring has been in existence for more than fifty years, and has done quite well. Anna is an accomplished seamstress and enjoys working for him. She has another part-time job in a millinery shop on Meeting Street. She specializes in alterations of suits and dresses.

The bell on the front door rings and Anna emerges from the back room.

"Hey Anna, huh you is?" the man at the door says.

"Benny?" she says, walks over and gives him a hug.

"I's jis pass'n' by an' stop to gib yah something like I tell yah I go do, 'membuh?"

"Oh yeah, I 'membuh."

"Is you hey by yahself?" Benny whispers.

"Mr. Broadnax at de bank. You ent workin' t'day?"

"I sta't early dis morn'n' an' off already. I hab my friend Joe Brown wagon. Takin' some fiahwood to a customer on Smith Street."

"Benny, you a hard worker."

"I sab'in up to meke dat trip down to Bewfu't nex' mont'."

"Uh-huh. I kno' yah go do dat. I be to Wadmalaw nex' mont' to see y'all b'fo' yuh go."

"Das good."

"Benny, I gotta git out dere."

"I hea' 'e ruf'," Benjamin says.

"Uh-huh, uh-huh. Us kin ha'dly breathe ... stink like ga'bage in de alley, 'specially aftuh rain. Dat one reason I ent bring Jacob to Chass'tun yet," Anna says.

"Huh much longuh you go be all jam up in dat alley?"

"Six mo' mont' be' fo I moobe to Charlotte Street, not far from Leon Jr. Gotta sabe money — dat why I work two job now. On Sunday, I too tired to go to church. Dat ent good, but I ent go lie."

"I kno wuh yah talkin' 'bout, sistuh. When I off de waterfront, I res' up fuh a lil' while, den I out sellin' wood. I do dat eberyday 'cept Sunday. Anyway, I gotta go now."

"Uh-huh," she says. *Teke care, Benny!"*

# CHAPTER 32

J acob finishes raking the yard and admires how neat the lines in the dirt look. They aren't deep in the winter because the ground is hard. But in summer he rakes more artistic lines. He sees images in the lines that no one else appreciates. Jacob walks to the side of the house, puts the rake in the shed and goes back to the front, tip-toes through his artwork and walks up the porch steps. He takes a deep breath and asks, *"Wuh yah cookin', Nana?"*

Mary, who is at the stove, puts the lid back on the big cast-iron pot. *"Rabbit stew."*

"Sho' smell good, Nana!"

Charlotte, sitting by the fireplace, tells Jacob, *"Mr. Sammy sent word yah momma go be hey soon."*

"Oh yeah, Auntie. I glad. Hope her got us a place in Chass'tun."

Mary smiles. *"I go meke sho' Anna hab nice place fuh yah b' fo' I let yah go."*

Later after supper, Jacob asks his grandmother, *"Nana, huh I git muh special name?"*

"Yah spirrut name?"

"Yes ma'am."

"From Afreeka ... de ol' folk say our people fust come hey cause dey be slabe. Dey ent wanna come buh dat wuh happ'n."

Jacob's eyes widen.

Mary continues. *"De ol' folk pass 'long eberyting dey 'membuh to dey chillum an' so on an' so fo'th. Dat why me an' yah grandaddy pass dem ting on to yuh. Dat so us 'membuh wey us be frum."*

"Oh, OK, Nana."

CHAPTER 33

I t's late March and the wind blows hard off the Atlantic Ocean. Charlotte has been busy packing for the move to Beaufort, and Anna has sent word she would be there on Mr. Sammy's boat that afternoon. Charlotte is excited, but also sad about leaving Wadmalaw. She stares out the window and reminisces.

"I lub dis house an' all de good membry. I tink 'bout Daddy puttin' me up in de big oak tree. Him say jump, girl, I ketch yah. So, I jis fall off de limb an' dat wuh him do. I ent nebuh go fuhgit dat, fuh tru." She looks over at her mother sitting in her rocker holding Sarah and singing softly. *"I go miss Momma too,"* she whispers to herself.

Meanwhile, Anna sits in the bow of the boat as Mr. Sammy rows into Wappoo Creek en route to Wadmalaw Island. They had left Charleston before the sun came up. Anna finished sewing dresses for Charlotte the night before and packed them along with two new shirts and two pairs of pants for Jacob. There's a hard chop on the creek now as they approach Elliott's Cut. Sammy locks down the oars and grabs the rudder.

"You OK, Anna?"

"I alrigh'."

"Good, now hol' on," he says as the boat is swept through the man-made cut into the Stono River. The tide is coming in and the wind is favorable. He unwraps the sail and the wind takes it. Moments later, Sammy tells his passenger:

"Anna, dey ent be no cut from the creek to the river a hundred yea' ago. A man name Mr. Elliott own all dis land round hey, and want to hook up Wappoo Creek wid de Stono Ribhuh. So he get dynamite and blow up de land. Dat why dey call 'um Elliott Cut. Sabe lotta time to get frum Chass'tun to Wadmalaw now."

"I glad he do dat," Anna says.

"I is too," Sammy says as he grabs a brown paper bag next to him.

"Go 'head Mr. Sammy, you eat while I row," Anna offers.

"No Anna, yah ent need to do dat," he replies with a hearty laugh. Wind got us now.

Anna smiles, and pulls a sandwich from her own bag as Sammy continues: *"I been talk'n' to a friend in Chass'tun 'bout dey son en daughtuh — boff 'bout yo' age. He say dey chillum gwine to Philly or maybe New York to work in a fact'ry. Ent kno' wuh kind ob fact'ry, buh 'e spose to pay good."*

"Uh-huh," Anna says. *"I ent wanna go to Philly or New York fuh work, buh I ent mind visit up dey someday."*

Sammy smiles. *"I ent wanna lib up dey either."*

They laugh as they finish their sandwiches and throw the crust to the gulls.

 **CHAPTER 34**

Jacob arrives home from school and hollers, *"Nana, yah want me to do anything?"*

Mary, sitting at the table cutting up okra, says, *"Get some wood fuh de stobe. I got cookin' to do."*

"OK, Nana," Jacob says and goes to the woodpile. He soon returns with an armful of short, seasoned oak for the stove. He has been thinking a lot about Emma lately. He imagines seeing her standing up front of a classroom teaching children, and looks forward to seeing her at Memorial Day festivities.

He walks into the yard and picks up the rake. He thinks about his grand-father, and the conversations they have had. There is not a day that goes by that he doesn't fidget with the button and a piece of the devil's backbone, both of which he carries in his pocket. He wishes he could tell someone about their powers, but he swore to Big Leon he wouldn't.

About that time, Mr. Sammy and Anna sail into the shallow Wadmalaw Sound.

"Benjamin tell me yah be look'n' fuh a new place to lib," Mr. Sammy says.

"Yes sir. I gwine git out from de alley I in now; gotta moobe s b'fo' Jacob come."

"I glad to hey dat," Sammy says. *"Dem alley nasty ... I kno' some folk dat ustuh lib back dey. Ent good. I go help yah wid dat ... go meke sho' yah alrigh' cause yah daddy wuh muh bes' friend, uh-huh."*

Tears well up in Anna's eyes. *"Tank yah, Mr. Sammy ... When 'e rain, dat alley flood, an' 'e stink bad back dere cause eberyting all back up. Rat big as rabbit running all round."*

Sammy lowers the sail and wraps it tight, then sets the oars. The boat is near the mouth of Bohicket Creek. He'll row the rest of the way to the landing.

# CHAPTER 35

Jacob is out front raking when a gust of wind rattles the palmettos. He turns his back to the wind, which is cool on his neck. He has felt this sensation before. Now he hears voices on the road, looks up and sees a man and woman walking his way.

"Hey, Jacob," his Uncle Peter calls out.

"I ent kno' yah com'n' t'day," Jacob says as he stares at the slender woman with his uncle.

"So dis be Jacob — de one dat ketch all dem big fush?" she says as they get closer.

"Das 'um," Peter says. *"Jacob, dis yah Aunt Mamie."* She gives the boy a hug. She is tall and her skin is lighter than Peter's. Her thick, black hair is braided down to her neck. Her voice is soft, somewhat squeaky, and her smile reminds Jacob of his mother.

"Yah uncle say yah kno' huh to ketch big fush."

Jacob smiles broadly.

Peter asks if Mary is home.

"Yes'sir. Nana go be surprise."

"Jacob, go 'head on in an' don' say nutt'n. Us be b'hind yuh," Peter says.

Jacob laughs, slaps his thigh, and says, *"OK, I go do dat!"* He walks slowly up the steps and into the house. Charlotte and Sarah are sitting by the fireplace and Mary is cooking at the stove.

"Hey Nana, wan' me to git anything fuh yuh?" Jacob asks.

"No, I got eberyting I need. I send yah out later fuh mo' wood."

"Alrigh'," Jacob says, smiling.

"Boy, why yah got dat big grin on yuh face? Wuh up?"

That's when Peter steps through the front door saying, *"Anybody home round hey?"*

"Oh my Gawd!" Mary says, as Mamie walks in behind Peter. *"So good to*

see yah girl. Huh yuh duh?"

"Ha! Dis sump'n," Peter says. *"I yah son buh yah skip me an' hug Mamie."*

Mary laughs. *"I see yah all de time. I ent see Mamie since I ent kno' when."*

Peter kisses Mary on her cheek and smiles.

"Wuh bring ya'll hey frum Edisto?" Charlotte asks.

"Us come to see yah b' fo' ya'll moobe to Bewfu't. Weh Sarah?"

"Obuh dey sleep'n."

Peter walks to the makeshift bed, leans down and gently rubs the side of the child's face with the backs of fingers.

"Sit down, ya'll," Mary says. *"Jacob, git me dat chair obuh dey so I kin sit too. Mamie, huh long yah go' be hey?"*

"Us leebe t'morruh when de tide back up."

"I got some tea on de stobe. Huh dat sound?" Mary asks.

"Sho' smell good," Mamie says. *"Wuh dat cookin'?"*

"Rabbit stew, an' I jis pull dis co'nbread out de oben … Want some wid yuh tea?"

"Yes ma'am."

"Me too Mama," Peter says.

Mary cuts several pieces of cornbread. *"Y'all wan' muhlassis an' budduh?"*

"No ma'am," they reply in unison.

She cuts a small piece for Jacob. *"Wash dem han' fust."*

Jacob goes out to the hand pump.

Peter and Mamie have been married for three years. Mary last saw her more than a year ago at a funeral. She likes Mamie but doesn't care for her family. Mamie is the youngest of four children. Their father left Edisto Island and never came back.

Mamie's mother and three aunts practice root medicine, and most folks fear them. But Mary knows Mamie has a good spirit.

"Charlotte, when yah gwine to Bewfu't?" Peter asks.

"Nex' week maybe."

"Benny skraight wid 'e new job?"

"Oh yeah, him teke care of dat, and find a place to lib too."

"Dat good. When y'all git settle, me an' Mamie go come see yah. I'll bring Momma an' Jacob too."

Charlotte and Mary nod in approval.

"Mamie, yuh look good," Mary says.

"Oh Miss Mary, I sho' is, 'specially aftuh yah tell Peter to bring dem leaf fuh me. I feel bettuh de nex' day. An' Peter put de sky blue paint round de winduh an' door. Aftuh him do dat a whole lotta ting change."

"Huh so?" Mary asks.

"Got lot mo' energy."

Mary smiles and nods.

Mamie continues, *"I go say dis — an' I ent nebuh tell Peter — yah son treat me real good Miss Mary. I kno' I dif'cult buh Peter neber git short wid me. Him calm me down an' alway say eberyting go work out jis' fine. Uh-huh. Peter tell me dat all de time, an' I glad I feelin' bettuh now."*

Peter smiles as Mary grabs her pipe, sits in the front room, lights up and says: *"Mamie, I so happy yah feelin' good. I pray fuh ya'll eberyday. Uh-huh, oh yeah!"* She looks up and raises her hand to the ceiling.

"Him a 'on time' Gawd," Mamie says. *"He go he'p yah when yah need 'um, dat fuh sho'."*

Mary smiles as she puffs on her pipe.

Mamie continues: *"I ent talk 'bout muh family much, but folk do say bad ting 'bout 'em. Some of all dat de trute ... dat meke me sad."*

"Mamie, Daddy usetuh say family can be yah worse enemy," Charlotte says.

"Uh-huh, fuh sho'," Mary says. *Peter, huh ting on Edisto?"*

"Good, Momma, us go send some cow to Savannah soon. I be back hey afta' dat and bring some yah some fresh meat. Dat remind me, I go look at yuh smokehouse b'fo' I go. Ent no need to bring yah meat if dat smokehouse ent right."

"OK, son, check 'um ... some meat in dey now buh not much."

Mary looks at Mamie and says, *"Las' time I see yah, yah look too thin ... Huh yah appetite?"*

"Whole lot bettuh now."

"Momma," Peter says, *"dis gal put down some food now."*

Mary laughs. *"Oh yeah. Das good."*

"Mamie eat'n' fuh two people," he adds.

Mary looks puzzled. Peter and Mamie smile.

"Lawd, Lawd," Charlotte shouts. *"Dey go hab a baby!"*

Mary jumps up, lifts her arms, and shouts, *"Oh JEDUS! JEDUS! JEDUS!*

Peter says, *"Yah go be a nana 'gain."*

Tears stream down Mary's face. *"Tank yah Gawd fuh ansuh'n muh prayer. Tank yah Jedus! Huccome you teke so long tell me? You sit in dis house drink tea, eat co'nbread an' ent say nutt'n 'bout dat."*

Mamie smiles and says, *"Uh huh, Miss Mary, us ent go say nuttin' at fu'st buh Peter say he go su'prise yah."*

"I too ol' fuh dem kinduh su'prise," Mary says. *"Huh much mont' you is?"*

"Three mont'."

Jacob isn't sure what the women are talking about.

"Wunda if dat baby go be like Jacob," Charlotte says. *"Jacob born wid de veil an' de birt'mark, an' yah don' play round wid dat."*

Peter stops laughing. Charlotte continues, *"Spooky Jacob hab dream 'bout fush, an' look at yah now!"*

Mamie smiles. *"Jacob dream 'bout me?"*

Mary turns to Mamie and asks, *"Peter ent tell yah 'bout Jacob gif'?"*

"Well, Peter say Jacob sometime skay Charlotte, but I tink 'e jokin'. Jacob too young to be spooky."

Charlotte looks at Peter. *"Huccome you tell Mamie I skay'd?"*

"I ent lie Sistuh! ... Momma, ent dat de trute?"

Mary laughs. *"Eberybody in de fambly kno' Charlotte sometime skay'd ob dat boy. Mamie kno' dat too now."*

"Don' talk 'bout me like dat," Charlotte says, *"I's yah favorite chil' ent I."*

"You is my skay'd chil'," Mary says, and everyone laughs. *"Now lemme finish wuh I say'n'. Mamie, dat boy dream a lot, an' wuh him dream 'bout off'un come to pass. Him can see and hea' spirrut too. Uh-huh, him sho' do!"*

Jacob smiles and thinks about how scared Charlotte would be if she knew he had been talking to Big Leon.

Later that day, Anna and Mr. Sammy arrive at the landing, where Mr. James waits patiently with his horse and wagon. Once Anna and her bags are on the wagon, Mr. Sammy returns to the boat and leaves for Johns Island. As he rows away, he waves. *"See yah later, Lawd will'n'."*

"Mr. James," Anna says, *"I 'preciate yah pickin' me up today."*

"No problem, Anna, I back an' fo'th like dis all de time. Huh yah trip from de big city?"

"Bin good. Me an' Mr. Sammy git to talk'n' an' b'fo us kno', hey we is."

"Well, I glad to hea' dat."

"Huh Miss Bertha doin'?" Anna asks.

"Her good ... right dey fuh me all de time."

They laugh as they cross the bridge then Mr. James says, *"Jacob an' yah momma go be glad to see yah."*

"Uh-huh. Momma go say her glad I come to see she in her ol' age," Anna says with a laugh.

"She say she gettin' ol'?"

"Das wuh 'e mout say — soundin' tired an' all dat — befo' her start laugh'n'."

"All Mary and Big Leon chillum turn out good," Mr. James says. *"Ya'll stick wid yah momma; Big Leon smil'n' down fuh dat."*

"Tank yah, Mr. James. Us try to do wuh right an' 'membuh wuh Momma an' Daddy tell us:

'Keep on do wuh yuh do, an' de Lawd go bless yah!'"

As they arrive at Mary's house, Mr. James hollers: *"Huh hunnuh fuh duh?"*

Mary comes to the door and waves. James helps Anna down from the wagon. She takes a silver dollar from her pocket, gives it to him, then hurries up on the porch and gives her mother a hug. Mary tells James, *"Hunnuh fuh duh … Gawd bless and tank yah!"*

"Yah welcome, Mary."

Jacob steps out on the porch and Anna throws her arms around her son.

"Ya'll go on inside," Mary says. *"Peter in dere wid Mamie, and dey say dey go hab a baby… Jacob, go get yo momma's bag."*

James and Anna burst out laughing about the news that Mamie is pregnant as Jacob grabs his mother's bags and returns to the porch. He stops, looks back and sees the lines he carefully created while raking are covered with horse and wagon tracks and footprints of people he loves. Inside, he hears his mother say, *"Look'a my baby brudduh Peter… he-self go be a daddy… Go on, Petee, and you too, Mamie!"*

"Sistuh," Peter says to Anna, *"yah look tired."*

Anna removes her coat and hat. *"Dat cause I is. Bin workin' hard. Got two job now… all dat water frum hey to Chass'tun mek me tired too."*

"Das de trute, Sis," Peter says. *"Gotta git all buck-up fuh dat long boat ride, and now yah hey."*

Mary places the palm of her right hand on Anna's forehead.

"I alrigh', Momma, I jis tired," Anna says.

"Uh-huh, I go meke some hot tea an' warm up yah bone."

"Yes ma'am, tank yah."

As Mary stands at the stove she says: *"Jacob dream 'bout fush, an' I tell Charlotte dat mean somebody in dis family go hab a baby. An looky hey who come t'day an' say dey wuh dey say, tank Gawd."*

"*Hush yah mout' Momma!*" Anna says.

Mary raises her right hand: "*Fuh true, Anna, fuh true!*"

"*Das right, Anna,*" Charlotte says.

"*Momma,*" Anna says, "*I 'membuh yah tell'n' me 'bout people dat dream ting like dat… den Jacob arribe.*"

"*Oh yeah, dat boy been dream'n, buh him ent say much 'bout 'um,*" Mary says.

"*Momma,*" Anna whispers. "*Peter an' Mamie go hab boy or girl?*"

Mary rubs her chin. "*I ent kno'… kinduh tricky. De wey 'e look right now, I tink her go hab a boy, buh I ent kno fuh sho'.*"

Mary walks behind Mamie, who is sitting on the couch, and rubs her daughter-in-law's shoulders.

"*I pray de baby be healthy. Dat all I ax fuh right now.*"

"*Tank yuh, Miss Mary.*"

"*Chil', stop call me 'Miss Mary.' You muh daughtuh too. Call me Momma.*"

Anna and Charlotte smile.

CHAPTER 36

"*So Anna, huh ting in de city?*" Peter asks as everyone sits in the front room.

"*Some folk leebin' Chass'tun — gwine to New York, Bal'imo'e, Philly — dey say good job up dere.*"

"*Yeah, dat wuh I hea' too,*" Peter says. "*A fella I kno' say de pay be good buh de winter ent.*"

Anna nods in agreement. "*I ent go up dey an' git all cramp up, an' cold … I ent gwine do dat.*"

"*Das right, Sistuh,*" Peter says. "*I tell dat fella de same ting … When de las' time you talk to Leon Jr.?*"

"*Yistiddy… Him stop by de sto' to meke sho' I OK.*"

"*Dat good.*"

"*Uh-huh. I tell Leon I olduh buh 'e like muh big brudduh. Leon ent go haffa worry wid me much longer 'cause annuduh man coming… Ent dat right Jacob?*"

Jacob smiles. "*Das right. When I git dey, ent nobody go mess wid muh Momma.*"

Charlotte, who is in the bedroom, hollers, *"Lawd hab mussy!"*

"Uh-huh," Peter says. *"Me an' Leon hab talk wid Jacob 'bout being man ob de house. If Mamie hab a boy, I go tell 'um: 'Boy, time go come when yah gotta act like a man an' stop all dat play'n. Teke care yah wife an' chillum; be de man in yah house; stand in de gap when dey need yah; and all like dat.' Das wuh muh daddy tell me."* Peter takes a deep breath and points down at Jacob, who is near the front door. *"Yah lis'nin'?"*

"Yes sir."

Charlotte walks out of the bedroom and asks, *"Anna, is yah talk to Benny lately?"*

"Uh-huh. Benny at muh shop las' week, an' left wuh in dat bag fuh you an' Sarah."

Jacob smiles and goes out front. Peter follows, saying, *"Jacob, I go teke dem rotten boa'd off Nana smokehouse an' put new ones on now."*

"Need help Uncle Peter?"

"Not right now, Jacob."

Back inside the house, Anna asks her mother what's cooking on stove.

"Rabbit stew."

"Dat mek me hongry," Anna says.

"Das wuh rabbit stew s'pose to do," Mary says.

Anna lifts the big pot lid, takes a deep breath and smiles. *"Leon Jr. say him go be hey next mont'."*

"Huh him doin', an' how dat some-timey wife ob his?"

"Momma, don' say dat 'bout Hazel," Charlotte says.

"Her am some-timey. I ent lie," Mary replies.

Anna tries to change the subject: *"Leon got anudduh boat, an' him got a dozen men work wid him now. Dey ketch lotta fush. Daddy be proud."*

"Das good, Anna, an' huh him wife do?" Mary asks again.

"I guess her alrigh'... I see Hazel in church buh dat 'bout it."

"Uh-huh," Mary says. *"Sump'n ent right wid dat gal. Her ent nuttin' like yah Aunt Mamie ... When I fust meet Mamie, my spirrut meet her too. Mamie got sweet spirrut."*

"Das right, Momma. She sho' do."

STANDING IN THE GAP

CHAPTER 37

Peter hangs two salted hams and a side of venison on hooks for curing inside the smokehouse. He brought the meats to Wadmalaw along with lumber and nails to repair the old building but didn't tell his mother. He wants to surprise her. He looks out into the yard at Jacob, who is busy with a rake working the sand.

Meanwhile, inside house, Mary, Mamie, Emma and Charlotte are still talking:

"Momma, I tink somethin' bothering you," Charlotte says.

"Uh-huh, an' I go tell yah, but please keep 'um to yuhself, OK?"

Charlotte, Mamie and Anna nod in agreement.

"Dis 'bout Emma," their mother continues.

"Wuh 'bout Emma?" Anna asks.

"Yah 'membuh wuh I say 'bout she momma Lizzy?"

"Yeah, dat Lizzy drop dead soon aftuh Emma born," Anna says.

"Uh-huh, I 'membuh you say dat, too," Charlotte adds.

"Uh-huh. Well, dat ent so," Mary says. *"When Lizzy pregnant wid Emma, Lizzy momma send her to Bewfu't to stay wid she fambly til aftuh her baby born."*

"Huccome?" Mamie asks.

"Lizzy wuh foolin' round and word get out 'bout her condition. Her momma tell Lizzy she gotta go away. Her say Lizzy can come back aftuh de baby born, and stan' in front of eberybody in de church an' apologize 'bout wuh happen. Well, Lizzy ent fuh dat. Her say ent kno' way she go tell eberybody 'bout dat baby... Uh-huh. Well, Lizzy hab Emma den tell she momma her ent wan' dat chil'. So she momma ax she friend Miss Geneva, who lib in Bew'fut, to take de baby an' tell eberybody dat Emma her own chil'. Miss Geneva say OK cause she ent got no chillum. Aftuh all dat, Lizzy moobe to Savannah, git marry and hab three mo' chillum. All dat time go by and Emma ent kno' Lizzy she real momma."

Anna drums her fingers lightly on the table then asks, *"Wey Emma daddy?"*

"Dey sent dat boy up Nort' to work, an' 'e ent nebuh be back. Nobody say nuttin' 'bout him no mo'."

"I go change de subject," Anna says, gets up, grabs two of her bags, gives one to Charlotte and the other to Mary. Charlotte opens hers first and removes

several new dresses — two for church and two more for daily wear, Anna says. Charlotte also pulls out four infant dresses and two bonnets for Sarah.

"Dese bootiful," Charlotte says while holding the soft cloth of one of the infant dresses against her cheek. *"Tank yah Anna!"*

"Glad yah like 'em. Dat cloth yah feelin' on yah face, Benny pick dat out. An' de cloth fuh yah dress, him pick dat out too."

"Well, hush muh mout'," Charlotte says. *"Him did dat fuh me?"*

"Un-huh," Anna says adding, *"OK Momma, open yuh bag now."*

Mary reaches in and pulls out a beige dress with a light-blue flower design.

"Ooowee! Dat go look nice on yuh," Mamie says.

"Yah teke dem word out my mout'," Mary says beaming. *"Dis purty. I go wear 'um Sunday."*

Mary reaches back in the bag and finds a blue hat trimmed in white lace with brown speckles in the pattern. She tries it on, walks back and forth and twirls like a model at the end of a fashion-show runway.

"Sump'n else in dat bag," Anna says.

Mary reaches back in, pulls out a can of Prince Albert pipe tobacco and says, *"Daughtuh, I feelin' like dis my birthday wid all dese nice ting yah gib me."*

Anna turns to Mamie and says, *"Stan' up fuh a minute sistuh … lemme see if dis one fit yah."* She removes a dress from another bag and holds it in front of her sister-in-law. *"Uh-huh… dis go work. Slip 'em on. Lemme see…"*

Mamie smiles and pulls the dress down over her head.

"Lil' long in de back," Charlotte says.

"Uh-huh," Anna says. *"I git muh sewin' kit an' fix dat quick."* She opens her suitcase and removes her sewing bag and measuring tape.

"Wait Anna… Don' do nutt'n yet," Mary says.

"Wuh wrong?"

Mary reaches over by the fireplace, grabs a broom, pulls out a thick reed of straw and says, *"Mamie, put dis in yah mout — let 'um hang out dey on de side."*

Mamie slowly puts a piece of straw in her mouth.

"OK Anna, go 'head," Mary says.

"Huccome yah tell Mamie to put dat in she mout'?" Charlotte asks.

"Gal, wuh wrong wid yuh! Like I done tell yah long time ago, don' nebuh stitch no cloth when yah got 'um on widout a piece wood in yah mout'. An' specially if yah wid chil'."

"Wuf-fuh Momma?" Charlotte asks.

"Dat bad luck. Das wuf-fuh."

"Momma, I ent nebuh hey dat b' fo'."

"I ent nebuh hey dat too," Mamie says laughing.

That's when Anna says, *"I fix a lotta dress on folk. Ent nobody hab nuttin' in dey mout' when I do. If I tell 'em to put stick in dey mout', dey tink I crazy!"*

Later that evening the temperature drops and everyone except Mary and Anna turn in. Makeshift beds are set up near the fireplace. Mary sits at the table and lights her pipe. The oil lamp flickers. Anna sits next to her mother.

"Momma, Jacob growin' fas' an' I ent round him like I spose to be. Jacob need to moobe soon to Chass'tun wid me."

"Gawd go teke care you an' Jacob," her mother says. *"Keep 'um in yah prayer an' yah heart."*

"Yes ma'am," Anna says then goes to bed.

Mary sits by herself for a while longer and thinks about the possibility of Jacob leaving Wadmalaw Island. She knows it would be best for him to be with his mother, and she accepts that she'll probably be living alone someday. After a few final puffs, she stands and takes the flickering lamp to her bedroom. Little did she realize at the time that almost all the folks still living on the Gullah and Geechee islands will face a similar reality: There are no jobs now for young people on the islands and that won't change. In time there won't be any of the "old folk" left.

 CHAPTER 38

It has been months since Anna, Mamie and Peter left Wadmalaw. Benny quit his job and joined Charlotte and Sarah at Mary's house, and for two days they have been packing their belongings for their move down to Beaufort.

"T'morruh de big day," Mary says sadly as she sits at the table skinning carrots and potatoes.

"Yeah Momma, dis bin a long time comin'. I kno' yah ready fuh us to git out yuh house."

"You ent in my way," Mary says barely above a whisper.

"Momma, us go come back, an' us go teke yah to Bew' fut to visit us."

"I ent wanna be a burden," Mary sighs.

"Mary Logan, you ent no trouble. Huh! If ent be fuh you, I ent kno' wuh I do." Charlotte takes her mother's left hand. *"Us also go mek sho' yah see Sarah grow up."*

"Well, das good, Charlotte," Mary says and finishes peeling the vegetables.

Everyone is up early the next morning. But Benjamin, Mary, Charlotte, Jacob and even little Sarah are silent as if each is not sure how to say good-bye. Mary had slept little, arose before the sun did, fired the wood stove and knelt in prayer, asking God to watch over her loved ones and for her own strength in dealing with loneliness in times ahead. She prayed so long her knees throbbed — so much so that she could hardly get back up.

Benjamin and Jacob wasted no time carrying everyone's bags to the landing, where William and Jeremiah wait with the boat for the long ride down the coast to Beaufort. Back at the house, Charlotte hands Sarah to Mary and says, *"Gib yah granny a hug, baby, 'e time to go."*

"Charlotte, yah mekin' me cry," Mary says. *"Ya'll go on now. I too sad to talk."*

"I teke good care of yuh daughtuh an' yah gran'," Benjamin vows. *"Us go hab a good life, and we comin' back soon to see yah."*

Mary manages a smile. *"Yah like a son to me, Benny. Gawd bless yah!"*

Benjamin takes Sarah in his arms. *"Let's go Charlotte, us got a long way to go.*

 # CHAPTER 39

Weeks later Mary sits alone rocking slowly by the fireplace. *"Too quiet jis sitt'n' hey,"* she whispers to herself. A northeast wind rattles the windows and the fire crackles. She closes her weary eyes and, somewhere between rattling and crackling, she hears familiar voices — sounds of laughter and songs that somehow linger.

"Seem like jis the oduh day dat me, Big Leon, an' de chillum bin up in hey. Now dey all gone … jis Jacob an' me now. Soon he be gone, too."

Meanwhile in Charleston, Anna is looking forward to moving into a house on Elizabeth Street on the east side of the city. It will soon be available for $30 a month. Tuberculosis — a contagious lung disease also known as "consumption" — is spreading through the city. Two of her neighbors in the damp alley where she currently lives were recently admitted to the Colored Hospital, where almost all the beds are filled.

Anna has been coughing for two weeks and is easily fatigued. She has treated herself with a wildflower tea called "Life Everlasting," which she brought back from Wadmalaw. She also mixes a touch of kerosene with a teaspoon of sugar for her throat. That's what her mother gave the children for colds. She worries about her health now — the sooner she moves, the better.

CHAPTER 40

"*Hey Jacob, pull dat anchor. Time to go,*" Mr. James says. They've been on the creek for more than an hour and the sun has yet to rise. The oil lamp in the boat is still lit as they row past the village at Rockville toward Jalapa Island. Most older islanders, including Mary, won't go near Jalapa. Older folks say it is inhabited by spirits, some good, some bad. As their boat nears the island, Jacob recalls the strange feeling he had the last time he was in the area. Now, as the sun emerges, they pass the big bend in the river where Jalapa appears in a foggy haze off the port bow. Sammy extinguishes the light in the oil lamp and the boat slows to a stop at the mouth of a tiny creek that twists back behind the island.

"*Us go stop hey, Jacob, fuh bait. Ease de anchuh down … don' want to scay off de fush,*" Mr. James says.

"*Yes sir.*"

As the anchor line tightens, the boat turns bow first into the mouth of a side creek and stops.

"*OK, Jacob, grab dat net, go to the bow an' throw 'um.*"

Jacob stands with net in hand, puts a part of the bottom of it in his teeth, then sails it sidearm while releasing it from his mouth. The net spins open six feet wide and lands in the mouth of the creek. As the weights settle to the bottom, Jacob gives the rope, which is tied to his left wrist, a quick jerk, and pulls everything in toward the boat. He feels the weight of his catch almost immediately and the net surfaces below his feet.

"*Good job, Jacob, bring 'um in de boat,*" Mr. James yells. "*Great Gawd! Dat net full a mullet. Get 'em in… das right … Now drop 'em in de bucket, uh-huh, das right!*"

But Mr. James isn't the only one Jacob hears hollering. As the boy empties the net over the bucket, he hears a cacophony of deafening shrieks — and they aren't coming from the mullet. Jacob looks up and all around but sees no one except Mr. James, who is busy grabbing fish that missed the bucket and flap around on the boat bottom.

The shrieks get louder but Mr. James is oblivious to them. Jacob sits down and shakes his head, trying clear his brain. A blast of hot air washes over the back of his neck. He tries to stand but can't.

"Moyo Samba … Moyo … help us please!" Jacob hears someone — or something — say.

"Uh, yes sir," Jacob replies.

"Jacob, wuh wrong," Mr. James asks.

"I ent kno' Mr. James, I whoozy."

Jacob's knees buckle and he almost falls out the boat. Mr. James grabs him by the back of his pants and sits him down. Jacob takes a deep breath, stands up and prepares to throw the net again.

"Jacob, yah almos' go obuhboa'd. Sit back down while I pull de anchuh," Mr. James says. *"Us ent need no mo fush; we gwine back to the landing."*

Jacob says nothing to Mr. James or anyone else that day about what he had heard from Jalapa Island.

 # CHAPTER 41

It's May on Wadmalaw. Mary and Jacob have been in the garden for almost two hours picking field peas, which they will put up for the winter. As they sit on the porch preparing to shell the peas, Mary sees a man walking across the yard. As he gets closer, she says:

"Leon Jr.? Wuh bring yah hey dis morning?"

"Hey, Momma." Leon stops at the bottom of the porch and manages a smile.

"Hey Uncle Leon. Huh you is?" Jacob asks.

Leon walks up the steps and grabs Jacob's right hand and gives him a big shake. *"Yah got some muscle on yuh bone now."*

"I been out wid Mr. James ketch'n fush an' swimps. I learn huh to cast a net, an' him lemme row de boat too."

"Mr. James let you do all dat?"

"Uh-huh. He got de arthuritis in 'e hand. So I he'p 'um."

"Leon," Mary says. *"Come on in de house an' I fix yuh some hot tea."*

Leon sits and the table and Mary pours him a cup of tea.

"Yah mus' tired comin' all de way from Chass'tun so early in de mornin'," she says.

"Jis a lil', Momma," he says as he takes a small package out of his bag and sits it on the table. *"I bring dis fuh yah."*

"Wuh dis is?"

"Dat mo' baccuh."

"Tank yuh, son. I almos' out."

Leon drinks his tea quietly while Mary works at the stove. After a while she says:

"Brekwus ready! Jacob come to de table, almos' time fuh yah to go."

"Weh yuh goin'?" Leon asks.

"Gwine fush'n' by Tickle Up Bridge."

"Dey still some good bass in dere?" Leon asks.

"Oh yeah," Jacob says, smiling, "and flounda too."

"I go fry 'um up fuh Sistuh Ella," Mary says.

"Hmmm," Leon says as he looks over at Jacob. *"Yah de man of de house now, huh?"*

"I guess so," Jacob says. *"I jis do wuh Nana tell me."*

Leon, obviously deep in thought, says nothing in response as Jacob eats breakfast. Minutes later, Jacob excuses himself, grabs his hat and heads out the door. *"Be back aftuh while wid Miss Ella fush."*

Moments later Mary sits next to her son and says, *"Leon, I kno' yah ent come all de way frum Chass'tun so early dis mornin' jis to bring yah momma some 'bacca. Wuh wrong?"*

He takes Mary by the hand. *"Momma, I got somethin' to tell yuh."*

"Wuh?"

"Anna in de hospital an' her ent good."

"Wuh wrong wid Anna?"

"Dr. Johnson say her got 'sumption."

"Wuh dat is?"

"Anna cough up blood an' short a breath, ent eat much, an' she weak and all like dat."

Mary says nothing.

"Momma, yah unduhstan' wuh I tell'n yuh?"

She remains quiet.

"Dr. Johnson say Anna catch de 'sumption frum somebody," Leon says. He doesn't tell her tuberculosis can be fatal or that visitors can only see their sick loved ones through a glass window at the hospital.

"Momma, doctor say her go hab to stay dere fuh while."

"Uh-huh," Mary whispers.

"Anna ent go come to Wadmalaw til her get bettuh. Ent kno' how long dat go be."

"Well, son, I goin' to Chass'tun."

Mary has never been to Charleston before. She has never wanted to. But things have changed.

# CHAPTER 42

Anna knew something was wrong long before her brother did. In early April she was walking home from work and saw her neighbor, Miss Brown, sitting on a wooden box at the entrance to the alley where they live. Miss Brown often sat there selling dried flowers.

"Las' time us talk you ent so good in de eyes — dey weak — an' yah loss weight," she told Anna.

"Well, I feel tired all de time. I work'n' two job an' by de time I git home, I too tired to fix dinnuh. I jis go to bed."

"Baby, yah gotta eat to keep up yah skrengt'," her neighbor says.

Anna coughed and said, *"Yes ma'am."*

"Oooh, chil', dat coughin' ent good! Sump'n bad goin' round. Yah see dat doctuh yet?"

Indeed, Anna has not been sleeping well. The night before, she woke up coughing and soaked in sweat. *"Yah right, Miss Brown ... sump'n ent right."*

Anna spent the next two days in bed with a fever and headaches. Her roommates were concerned but thought she would be OK after some more rest. On the third day, Anna woke up when she heard: "BAM, BAM, BAM!" Someone was at the door.

Anna went to see who was there.

Miss Brown and Dr. Johnson were outside her apartment. *"Anna, Anna,* Mary Brown says. *Open de door! I got de doctuh hea wid me."*

Anna opens the door.

"Hey Miss Anna," Dr. Johnson says. *"How yah feelin'?"*

"I ent good," Anna says as he helps her back into the bedroom. *"Muh head hurt an' muh t'roat sore. I hot wid de febuh too."*

"Uh-huh," Dr. Johnson says. *"Miss Brown will help you get dressed. We're going to the hospital."*

# CHAPTER 43

A nna didn't remember anything after that. When she came to her senses, she was in a single bed in a large room that was fresh and clean. Lots of other beds with other folks were in the room too. Several nurses were busy changing sheets and tending to patients. Her headache was gone but she still had a fever. A sheet was wrapped tight around her. She tried to roll over but couldn't, so she closed her eyes again, too weak to move. After a while she hears a voice:

"Anna, do you know who this is?"

She opens her eyes and sees Dr. Johnson.

"Yes sir, I kno' who you is."

"You're in the hospital, and you'll be here for a while. OK?"

"Huh long I bin hey?"

"Almos' a week… You're in the Colored Hospital. Miss Brown has your clothes so don' worry 'bout 'em.

Dr. Johnson and a nurse check Anna's heartbeat and temperature and other vital signs.

"Anna, I'll explain this bes' I can," the doctor says. *"A sickness has been going around for at least six months. It's called "consumption." Heard of it?"*

"I ent kno' wuh dat is."

"Well, it's when you have a real bad cough and steady fever. Anybody where you live been sick like that?"

"Uh-huh. Two people in muh buildin' been sick like dat… ent kno' wuh happen to 'em."

"Uh-huh," Dr. Johnson says. *"Consumption is contagious. It passes from one person to the next, usually through sneezes and coughs. It gets into the air and spreads. You're going to have to stay here until it clears up."*

Anna listens quietly. Leon Jr. heard his sister was sick, checked with Dr.

Johnson about the prognosis and left in one of his fishing boats well before sunrise for Wadmalaw to tell their mother.

"Momma, Dr. Johnson say yah can see Anna whenever yah wannuh" Leon tells his mother. *"I gotta go back to de city dis aftuhnoon. Sammy say yah can ride wid him to Chass'tun next week, and I teke you to see Anna. Yah can stay at my house as long as yah like."*

His mother says nothing, thinking about Anna being in the hospital and wondering how long it will take before her daughter is released.

"Well," Mary says after a while, *"I go nex' week. Jacob can stay wid Peter and Mamie.*

"OK, Momma," Leon Jr. says. *"I'll get word to Peter 'bout all dis."*

 # CHAPTER 44

A week passes since Leon Jr.'s surprise visit to Wadmalaw. Mary is set to leave for Charleston with Mr. Sammy in the morning, and Jacob has moved to Edisto Island to stay with Uncle Peter and Aunt Mamie. Mary told Jacob his mother was in the hospital but gave no details. Now she sits quietly with her packed suitcase in the main room of her house reminiscing about all the good times her family had enjoyed there. She has prayed day and night for strength and guidance. The silence is broken:

"Hey dey, hunnuh. Huh yah fuh do?" Mr. James hollers from his wagon out front. Mary steps out the porch:

"Hey, Brudduh James. I ready."

James walks across the yard and onto the porch. *"Eberyting go work out, Sistuh, good Lawd willin'.* He carries her bag to the wagon then helps Mary up on the seat. As the wagon leaves the yard, she says, *"Dis de fust' time ent nobody stayin' in muh house."*

"Don't worry 'bout yuh house. I check on 'um. I go mek sho' eberyting OK, and I feed dem chicken and pig too," Mr. James says.

Neither he nor Mary say anything until they arrive at the landing, where Mr. Sammy is standing on the dock and a young man waits in the boat.

"Huh ya'll fuh do?" Mr. Sammy asks.

The young man gets out of the boat and walks up to the wagon.

"Dat muh nephew, Joe," Mr. Sammy hollers.

James and Mary are out of the wagon now, and Joe grabs Mary's suitcase. Later, after Mary gets settled in the boat, Joe loosens the dock line. Mr. James waves and says, *"Keep de Lawd first — he teke care ob dis fuh yah."*

"Tank yuh James," Mary replies. *"I go 'membuh wuh yuh tell me, an' I be skrong."*

Mary, her heart raging, sits in the bow, Joe takes up the oars, Sammy is in the stern, and off they go.

"Me an' Joe go gib' yuh a smooth ride to Chass'tun, Mary, so relax," Sammy says.

Mary nods but says nothing.

 CHAPTER 45

Two hours later, the sun rises as the trio ride up the Stono River towards Charleston. Mary has said nothing since they left the dock.

"Sistuh Mary, is you OK?" Mr. Sammy asks.

"I alrigh'," she says with a yawn.

Joe smiles and says, *"Teke a nap if yah wannuh."*

"I ent go sleep… might fall out de boat, an' wey too much water in dis ribuh fuh me to swalluh."

The men chuckle, and Mr. Sammy says, *"Sistuh Mary, dey mo' people in Chass'tun den yuh eber see b' fo'. Dey walkin' an' ride'n' in dey wagon an' on de trolley too. Dey go be white folk ridin' round in dey car. All us got on Wadmalaw is one old beat-up truck."*

"Wuh all dem people do dere?" she asks.

"Wuh you talk'n 'bout, Sistuh … Dey is collu'd, white, young an' ol' in Chass'tun. Dey all obuh de place doin' dis an' dat. Some all mix up wid each udduh, uh-huh."

Mary sits quietly, thinking about all she has heard about the city and worrying about Anna. After a while Sammy says, *"De tide 'bout out now, an' us go hit 'em jis righ' to get to wey us is goin'."*

"Huh yuh kno' dat?" Mary asks.

"See dem seagull all round? When yah see 'em fly'n' high, 'e mean tide 'bout to come in. If dey fly'n' low like dey is now, de tide 'bout gone."

● CHAPTER 46

Leon Jr. and Hazel have been at the hospital for about an hour mostly looking through a huge glass window at Anna, who is in one of numerous beds on the other side. Hazel was reluctant to be there for fear of getting sick. She has walked past the hospital before but has not been inside until now. She takes hold Leon's hand as a nurse helps Anna into a sitting position then rolls the bed over to the glass petition. Anna manages to smile when she recognizes Leon and Hazel. Leon places his right hand up on the glass and holds it there. Anna lifts one of her hands about halfway then puts it back down slowly.

"Please git bettuh," Hazel tries to tell her through the thick glass as Anna closes her eyes and drifts off to sleep.

"Wonduh wuh her tink'n' 'bout?" Hazel asks.

The nurse wheels Anna back to her place. Leon and Hazel stare for a while then leave. When they get to the lobby Leon sees Dr. Johnson.

"Hello Dr. Johnson, dis my wife, Hazel."

"How you do, ma'am?"

"Fine, tank you."

"Walk with me," the doctor says as they go back upstairs to the room with the glass petition. *"Anna doing better today, but she must stay a while longer. Some folks in there been here for three months and more."*

"Why dey in dey so long?" Hazel asks.

"Depends on the patient," he says. *"Anna has to breathe on her own, have no fever and be able to walk on her own before she can leave."* The doctor places a hand on Leon's shoulder: *"Your sister is making progress. The next thirty days will be critical. If we can get her lungs clear and her appetite returns, she has a good chance of leaving."*

About an hour later, Leon and Hazel are walking back home. *"Momma spose to arrive dis aftuhnoon,"* Leon says. *"I hope dey catch de tide on time."*

Hazel says nothing.

"Wuh wrong Hazel?"

"Ent nuttin'. I'll hab her room ready when Mary get to de house, Leon, I promise," she says. *"We go hab peas an' rice t'night."*

"Dat sound good, Hazel. Aftuh I walk yah home, I gwine to de Batt'ry an' wait fuh Momma."

CHAPTER 47

As Sammy's boat enters Charleston harbor from Wappoo Creek, Mary sees the wide cityscape. She's never seen anything like it, especially so many church steeples in one place. Charleston covers the southern portion of a peninsula between the Ashley and Cooper rivers, and numerous boats of various sizes are moving here and there in and around the harbor. As Joe rows parallel to Charleston's White Point Garden and enters the Cooper River, Mr. Sammy points to a man waving his arms at the corner of the High Battery.

"Look there on the wall. Dat Leon Jr. waving at us. See 'um ... see 'um! Dat Leon ... See 'um Mary? Dat yo' boy!"

Mary looks left toward the Battery and sees the man. *"I go take yah word on dat, Sammy,"* she says as the boat turns up the Cooper River toward the landing between the Custom House and the Market. Mary's heart beats like a battle drum as she struggles to catch her breath:

"Lawd, Lawd, please calm my soul an' gimme skrengt'," she prays quietly.

"You OK, Sistuh?" Sammy says.

"Uh-huh. I OK."

Joe rows hard to the landing until the boat scrapes bottom. He jumps out with bow line in hand and ties it to a nearby post. Leon, who had sprinted from the Battery wall up East Bay Street to the landing arrives and hurries down to the water.

"Hello everybody, huh ya'll do?" Leon says.

"Hey Leon," Mary says as her son grabs her around the waist, lifts her up and carries her to dry land. He puts her down, gives her a big hug and says, *"I sho' is glad yah hey Momma."*

CHAPTER 48

Jacob finishes his breakfast and helps Aunt Mamie clean up before he goes fishing in a nearby tidal creek.

"Jacob, watch yahself down by dat water," she says.

"OK Auntie, I go be careful."

Peter has told him about a good spot to catch bass where the dirt road turns alongside the creek. Jacob — with bait, a bucket and two fishing poles in hand — walks for about 20 minutes beneath large live oak trees with moss-draped limbs that form a canopy. He stops when he reaches a clearing at the bend in the creek. A slight breeze comes from the west and the tide starts to rise.

Jacob fishes for a while, then gets a strike — a nice bass, a pound or so. He removes the hook and drops the fish into his bucket, which he has filled with water and covered with an old board he uses for a seat. He baits the hook again with a strip of cut mullet, flips the line back into the water, sits down and thinks about his mother. He knows she's very sick. Otherwise, his grandmother would not go all the way to Charleston. He closes his eyes and, although he seldom asks God for anything, gives it a try.

CHAPTER 49

Leon Jr. and his mother walk a few blocks from the landing to the house on Chapel Street, where his wife Hazel is preparing supper and worrying. She is tired but determined to make a good impression on her mother-in-law. They have not been close because Hazel refuses to take the boat trip to Wadmalaw. Cars and bridges are few and deep water is more like a tall wall for folks who don't know how to swim.

As Leon Jr. and Mary reach Meeting Street she asks why the railroad tracks run down the middle of the paved road. Leon smiles and says:

"Dem track fuh de trolley, not a big train wid engine and de box car and de caboose an' all like dat. Folk ride de trolley all obuh town, getting' on an' off hey and dey wey'ebuh dey goin' to. See dem wire up obuh de track? Dat wuh moobe de trolley round town. Dat ting ent need coal; 'e run on 'lectricity — it like lightnin' in de wire and dat wuh meke 'um go. Dat wire hook on top de trolley and dat 'lectricity go down in dey an' turn dem wheel. Unduhstan' wuh I sayin'?"

Mary smiles knowingly: *"Son, I kno' 'bout 'lectricity. Someday dem pole and dat wire go be out to Wadmalaw an' folk go hab 'lectric light an' 'lectric stobe an all like dat. Buh I ent go be hey when dat happen. I go be up wey de lightin' come frum, Gawd willin'. I go be back en' Big Leon arm."*

As they continue along Meeting Street, Mary eyes the two- and three-story buildings, power lines, cars, trucks and more people that she has ever seen in one place at the same time. That's when Leon Jr. says:

"Muh fust time to Chass'tun, I do de same ting yah do right now: I lookin' all round at eberyting. Buh I get use to 'um aftuh while."

Mary tells her son in a low voice, *"I ent nebuh see dis much white people b' fo."*

He smiles and says, *"Oh yeah, lotta buckra hey. People frum all obuh de worl' work and lib in Chass'tun. In fac', some dem people dat look white be cullud ... Dey mix up."*

"I kno' 'bout dat too, son, like Mr. Jacob Flemming an' 'e chillum."

They walk another block and Leon says, *"Momma, us go turn hey ... dis Chapel Skreet. See dat grey house? Das it. Hazel waitin' fuh yah inside."*

Mary looks at the two-story house, and looks back at her son. Leon Jr. smiles. *"Momma, we ent lib in de whole house; we lib downstairs. De man dat own de house lib upstair."*

Leon sees a white woman sitting on the porch of house across the street.

"Hello, Miss Alexander," he tips his hat and says. She looks at Mary and nods her head without speaking.

"Hello Mr. Goldberg," Leon tips his hat again and says to a white man just inside the gate to the gray house.

"Hello Leon," he replies with a smile and tips his hat in return.

"Mr. Goldberg, dis is my momma, Mary Logan."

"How do, ma'am. Nice to meet you."

"Huh is you, sir?" Mary asks, wondering exactly who Mr. Goldberg is.

Leon, with Mary's bag in hand, walks up the front steps. *"Follow me, Momma."* He walks past the front and down a long side porch to the back and stops at the second door. *"Dis wey us lib, Momma,"* Leon says as he puts down the bag and opens the door. *Mr. Goldberg lib upstairs. He de landlord.*

CHAPTER 50

*"H*azel, we's come'n' in!"* Leon says as they step in the apartment. Hazel is in the kitchen, which has a table and chairs off to one side. She wears a brown-and-white cotton dress and a red apron. Her hair is tied with

a bright yellow-and-blue scarf.

"Hello, Leon; hello, Miss Mary, welcome!"

Hazel had rehearsed this moment for days hoping to make a good impression on her mother-in-law. Leon kisses his wife on the cheek and takes his mother's bag to the guest bedroom. Hazel reaches out with both arms to embrace Mary.

"It's has been a while," Hazel says.

Mary smiles and hugs her daughter-in-law.

"Please have a seat Miss Mary. It's a long way from Wadmalaw," Hazel says as she pulls out a chair.

Mary sits and rubs her knees. *"It sho' is Miss Hazel. Dat walk on dem ha'd skreet 'bout did muh knee in."*

"Miss Mary, I hope the weather gets warmer, so ol' Mr. Arthur Wrightus leaves yah alone."

Mary runs her right hand across the deep blue tablecloth, which drapes down to the oakwood floor. She notices that the walls are covered in white-and-blue paper. She has never seen wallpaper before. She notes that the fireplace is small, hardly big enough for a log, and wonders how her hosts stay warm at night.

Miss Mary, want something to drink? I'll make some tea," Hazel says.

"Jis water fuh now."

Hazel gets a glass from the cupboard and pours Mary some water from a pitcher near the sink. There is a knock at the door and Leon goes out to see who it is. Mary listens carefully and hears Leon say, *"No sir. No sir. Yes sir. I tink so."*

That's when Hazel says, *"You hungry, Miss Mary?"*

"I OK right now, Hazel. Wuh yah cookin'?"

"I have peas and rice, and boiled cabbage. I'll fry some fish too."

Mary sits up straight and looks at the pots on the stove. *"Huh yah mek yuh peas an' rice?"*

"I just heat them up. They were ready when I bought them."

"Wey yah get 'em already fix up?"

"From a man who comes around here with his cart. He's a street vendor."

"Uh-huh," Mary says.

Leon comes back inside and sits next to his mother.

"Who was at the door?" Hazel asks.

"Mr. Broadnax ax me to bring 'um thirty pound a fush by nex' week."

William Broadnax is one of several store owners who Leon supplies with fresh seafood. He has owned his store for years and sells porgy, bass, mullet, whiting, oysters, crabs and shrimp. He competes with numerous street vendors who buy seafood, meats and vegetables on the docks before making their rounds through the neighborhoods.

"Das a lotta fush," Mary says.

"No Momma, dat not a whole lot. Mr. Broadnax hab lots a customer."

Hazel smiles. *"I'll write his order in the book."* She learned accounting in school and also helps with the books at her uncle's lumber yard north of Charleston.

After a while Leon leaves to make a delivery. They ladies enjoy talking for hours until Hazel says:

"I'll fix dinner."

"Sound good to me… Wuh can I do to help?"

"Nothing, Miss Mary. I'm fine."

About an hour later Leon returns, puts a package in the sink and sits at the table next to his mother. Hazel lifts the lid on a cast iron pan that she's had on low heat. She gets three china plates from the cabinet, places them on the table, and fills each with peas and rice, a piece of fried sea bass and steaming cabbage.

After supper, Mary smiles and says, *"When yah say a man already cook dem pea and rice, I ent b'leeb yah. Wuh 'e name?"*

"Folks call him Hopp'n John because one of his legs is shorter than the other … when he walks he looks like he's hoppin'," she says with a laugh.

"Uh-huh," Mary says. *"Eberybody on Wadmalaw meke dey own rice and pea, specially on New Year Day. Hazel, dat suppuh wuh good. Dat cabbage tasty, an' yah fry dat fush jis right."*

"Thank you, Miss Mary," Hazel says. *Want tea?"*

"Jis a lil' bit.

Leon reaches into his coat pocket, pulls out a small paper bag and hands it to Mary.

"I got dis fuh yuh, Momma."

"Wuh dat is?" she asks as she eyes the little brown bag.

"Look see…"

She opens it and takes a deep breath.

"Some mo' Prince Albert 'bacca," Leon says.

"Tank yuh, Leon, buh I ent bring muh pipe."

Leon hands his mother a small wooden box.

"Wuh dis?" she asks as she opens the lid. Inside is a store-bought wooden pipe. *"Why yah hab dis pipe? It bran' new... Is yah smoke now?"*

"No ma'am. I got dat fuh yah. It cherry wood. I trade fush fuh 'um."

Mary takes the pipe from the box and places it on the table. It's deep red — darker on the top than on the bottom, smooth and polished.

"Momma, when yah finish yuh tea, come in de livin'room, sit by me an' smoke dat ting," Leon says as he points to a rocker next to the couch in the next room. Moments later Mary is sitting in the rocker and puffing away.

"Huh yuh like dat cherry wood?" Leon asks.

She takes another puff and smiles. *"Gotta get 'um broke in, son, b'fo' 'e jis' right."*

Hazel sits at the table and writes down orders for fish and shrimp in Leon's ledger. His business has picked up since he added another boat to the fleet.

"Anna go be glad to see yah, Momma," Leon says. *"Dr. Johnson say her gitt'n bettuh."*

"Wuh 'zactly wrong wid Anna, Leon?"

Hazel stands, walks over to the couch, sits next to Leon and says:

"Miss Mary, Anna has wuh is call consumption — it's contagious. If someone gets too close to her, she might get sick too. That's why she's in the hospital in a big room behind a glass window. Anna has bad a cough and trouble breathing. She'll be in that room til she ain't contagious no more. Unduhstand what I'm sayin'?"

Mary sighs and puts down her pipe. *"When Anna go git out?"*

"At least a mont'," Leon says.

"Uh, huh," Hazel adds. *"That's what the doctor said. We're going to see Anna tomorrow. You'll see what we're talking 'bout."*

"Das right, Momma, y'all go see Anna t'morrow. I go catch fush," Leon says.

"OK," Mary says, trying not to cry.

 # CHAPTER 51

It was still dark when Leon got up the next morning and left the house. Mary, who had a difficult time sleeping, is wide awake, worried about

Anna, wondering how Jacob is doing on Edisto Island. As the morning sun illuminates her bedroom, Mary gets out of bed and walks into the kitchen. Hazel stands by the stove preparing breakfast.

"Good morn'n' Miss Mary. Sleep good?"

"I toss an' turn… ent usetuh dat bed yet."

"Well, Anna will be glad to see yah this mornin'."

"OK, Hazel. I go wash up an' git dress. Sho' smell good in hey."

Mary gets dressed and sits at the table. Hazel fixes two plates for breakfast and sits across from Mary. She tells Mary about riding the trolley across town to the hospital, and what to expect when they get there. Mary warms up to her estranged daughter-in-law, is impressed with the way she keeps house and helps Leon Jr. Mary is reminded of when she was young and married to Big Leon.

"Hazel, wey us go get on dat trolley train?"

"At the corner of Chapel and Meeting streets. It's not far… let's go."

While walking to the stop, Mary says, *"Leon showed me dem track dat de trolley ride on down de middle ob de skreet."* The steel rails run down the middle of the street and several passengers have already gathered at the corner.

"Yes ma'am," Hazel says, *"the trolley will be here soon, and I have change in in my purse."*

"How much 'e cos'?" Mary asks.

"A nickel each."

Mary pulls out a dollar bill neatly folded into a square.

"No Miss Mary … I got it."

Three women and two men are waiting at the stop. Both of the black ladies exchange brief greetings with Hazel and Mary. The white woman and white men say nothing. Mary tries not to stare at the strangers.

"Trolley comin' now," Hazel whispers to Mary. The pavement starts to shake, the train rolls into view and squeals loudly as its metal wheels stop on the rails. Mary steps back on the wide slate sidewalk and eyes wires that extend from a rod atop the train to a thicker wire held up by street poles the length of the route. Hazel holds Mary's arm as all three white passengers board first, drop coins into a glass box beside the driver and sit up front. The others wait while Hazel helps Mary up the steps. Hazel drops two nickels into the box. *"Dis is for me and Mary,"* Hazel tells the driver, who eyes the glass box as the coins fall through a narrow hole to the bottom.

"We sit in the back, Mary," Hazel whispers, *"so watch your step. I'm right here behind you."* They sit in two seats in the back at the end of the aisle. The other two black women take the seats in front of Mary and Hazel.

"You OK?" Hazel asks Mary.

"Uh huh," Mary says as she sits nervously holding her pocketbook close to her chest. A sudden thrust of the train catches her by surprise. *"Ooooh, now dat sump'n."*

Hazel reaches over and holds her hand. *"Don't worry. Look around, enjoy yourself ... lot to see 'tween here and the hospital."*

At the next stop, a black woman gets on, sits across from Mary and places a large straw basket with a lid on the floor in the aisle. *"Huh hunnuh fuh do?"* she asks Hazel and Mary.

"Morn'n', Miss Lydia," Hazel says with a smile. Lydia is one of numerous street vendors who sell fresh vegetables, seafood, flowers and other items mostly between Broad and Calhoun streets downtown. She is best known for her deviled crabs.

"Miss Lydia, this my mother-in-law, Mary Logan, from Wadmalaw Island."

Lydia smiles, extends her hand and says, *"I hey good ting 'bout yah, Sistuh Mary. Leon an' Hazel go to de same church as me, an' dey good folk. Yah raised up Leon right. If he hab extra fush, 'e gimme some. Lawd bless Leon ... him gotta free hand."*

Mary smiles. *"Tank yah!"*

Hazel smiles too.

Lydia says to Mary, *"I got people that libbed near Rockville, buh dey on Edisto now."*

"Wuh dey name?" Mary asks.

"Bligen."

"Oh yea, I know dem Bligen. Dey be cuz'n on muh daddy side," Mary says.

"Dat mean us fambly," Lydia says with a laugh.

"Ent dat somethin','" Mary says.

"Sistuh, dat happ'n all de time round hey," Lydia says.

The trolley stops at the corner of Meeting and Broad streets. Miss Lydia stands and uses both hands to lift her basket off the floorboard. *"Dis muh stop, ladies. I got debil crab today, dey spice up right. Nice to meet yah, Cuz'n Mary... See yah in church if not b'fo'. You too, Sistuh Hazel."*

Hazel says to Mary: *"She makes the best devil crab you'll ever taste. That's what's in her basket. She sets up near de corner an' sells her crabs quick — two dozen or more a day. Sometimes she walks over to the Market an' sells 'em there too. De 'Crab Lady' — that's what folks call Sistuh Lydia."*

"Uh-huh," Mary says. *"I go hab to try some ob dat."*

"Yes ma'am, a lot a folks make a living round here selling fresh vegetables, peas, rice, crab, fish, shrimp. Fresh flowers too. Some push their carts up and down the streets and sing 'bout what they have to sell. That's how folks know they coming."

"Uh huh," Mary says. *"On de island, us ent sell much on the skreet. If somebody need sump'n, us gib it to 'um if dey 'nuf to go round. Mr. Sammy and Jacob sell fush and swimps and crab at de Bohicket landin' to folk dat teke 'em to Chass'tun in dey boat."*

Hazel smiles. *"Street sales are big business here."*

"Ting sho' different round hey," Mary says.

"That's right," Hazel says. *"Folks like Sistuh Lydia do good 'cause they tell all kinds of stories about this and that to customers. Lotta people listen close to what Lydia says 'bout the spirit world. She know all 'bout that."*

"Uh-huh," Mary says. *"Muh gran'son, Jacob, kno' 'bout spirrut too, buh e' ent say much."*

The women remain silent until the trolley arrives at the corner of King and Cannon streets not far from the hospital.

"OK Miss Mary, this is where we get off," Hazel says. Both women stand up and Hazel leads Mary to the rear exit. *"See the little shop with the red door? That's where Anna works."*

Mary looks down King Street. *"Sho' am lotta sto' on dis skreet."*

Hazel smiles broadly. *"They make lady's hats there. Anna sells 'em to women who stop in."*

"Uh-huh," Mary says. *"Anna gib me one dem hat las' time her on Wadmalaw. I wear 'um to church. She work pa't-time in dat sto' an' pa't-time somewhey else."*

Hazel and Mary walk west on Cannon Street, which is lined with wooden houses and corner stores. The houses are narrow across the front and very close to each other. Tall poles are spaced close to the sidewalk down the right side of the street. Attached to the poles are spiderwebs of electric wires.

"Walk on the sidewalk, Ms. Mary, an' be careful. Don't want no mud to splash on yah dress when a wagon or truck passes."

Several boys scurry down the sidewalk and one bumps Mary slightly as he runs past.

"Too many young'uns round loose round hey," Hazel says. *"Ain't got manners — almos' knock yah down buh don' crack 'e teete; don' say 'scuse me or nuttin'.*

"Why dey ent in school?" Mary asks.

Hazel shrugs her shoulders.

The women walk several more blocks toward the Ashley River and Hazel points to a three-story wooden building on the left. *"That's the Colored Hospital."*

"Dear Gawd, gimme skrengt'," Mary whispers as they arrive.

"Come on, Miss Mary, through this door," Hazel says as she takes hold of Mary's hand. They walk into a big room with a ceiling taller than any Mary has ever seen. Hazel points to woman sitting at a desk in a corner. *"Come on Mary, we go talk to her."*

"Good mornin'," Hazel says to the woman. *"We here to see Anna Rouse."*

"Good morn'n', Miss Hazel," the woman says. *"Sign in right here like you did before. Who is this lovely lady wid yah today?"*

"Dis Mary Logan ... She's Anna Rouse's mother."

"Nice to meet yah Miss Mary."

"Nice to meet yah too," Mary says.

Hazel signs in, grabs Mary's hand and they walk side-by-side down a long hall with rooms on both sides. Some of the doors are open, and Mary sees patients in beds and nurses inside. They stop at a huge room with double-doors at the end of the hall.

"This is where Anna is," Hazel says.

They walk through the big doors into a large space partitioned by a glass wall from ceiling to floor that has two more doors on the left. Mary looks through the glass at a dozen or so beds and the people lying in them. Nurses go in and out through the glass doors as they tend to their patients.

"That's Anna," Hazel says pointing to the front row of beds. *"She sittin' in a rolling chair next to her bed. See her?"*

Mary moves close to the glass, squints and sees the wheelchair.

"Excuse me. Excuse me," Hazel says as she taps on the glass. The nurse sees Hazel, turns the wheelchair around and pushes Anna towards the glass.

Mary's legs buckle, and Hazel grabs her arm. *"I got yah, Miss Mary — is yah alrigh'?"*

"Uh-huh," Mary whispers. *"Anna look thin."*

Anna manages a smile.

"Wuh happ'n to muh baby girl?" Mary says loud enough for Anna to hear

her though the glass.

"*Hello Miss Mary,*" a man who walks up behind the women says. Mary turns around and sees Dr. Johnson: "*I hope you brought me some of your shrimp perlo.*" He takes Mary by the hand and continues:

"*Miss Mary, Anna has a sickness called tuberculosis. It's very contagious — which means it is easily passed from one person to another. That's why your daughter is behind the glass. Don't want it to spread.*"

"*Hazel an' Leon say her got de 'sumption,*" Mary says.

"*Yes, it's known as consumption … also called TB,*" he explains. "In cities like Charleston, people live and work close to each other. If somebody has this disease and sneezes or coughs, it can pass through the air and infect others. It causes congestion in the lungs … makes it hard to breathe.

"*So yah gib Anna some medicine?*" Mary asks.

"*That's right. Anna needs a lot of rest and a proper diet too. That's why she's here. Anna's a good patient.*"

"*Huh long Anna go stay?*"

"*Four to six weeks, maybe more.*"

Mary turns and looks through the glass at her daughter, who manages a little smile.

"*But sometimes, Miss Mary, the patient doesn't make it,*" he continues. "*Sometimes their lungs get too congested. I'm glad we got Anna to the hospital as fas' as we did.*"

"*Tank yah, Dr. Johnson, fuh tek'in' care a muh daughtuh.*"

"*You welcome, Miss Mary, just keep prayin' for Anna.*"

"*Ent gotta worry 'bout dat, doctuh,*" Mary vows, then turns and places a hand on the glass.

Anna raises her hand, sits up a little and smiles. She gently lays her head back and lowers her arm as the nurse turns the chair and rolls her back to her bed.

 # CHAPTER 52

Mary says nothing during the ride back to Chapel Street until Hazel breaks the silence:

"*That's the Market, Miss Mary. It's where Leon sells mos' of his catch. The men go out in the ocean in their boats. Sometimes they row; sometimes they sail.*"

Ain't nutt'n but water out past the jetty rocks."

The train stops at the Market and a multitude of folks shop and work in and around a long line of gray sheds under which local vegetables, meats and other items are sold. Large turkey vultures line the crest of the meat shed waiting for scraps tossed into the street.

"Wey all dem buzzard come from?" asks Mary.

"From all round here," Hazel says, *"and they leave nuttin" in the street by time the sun sets."*

" Bad luck when buzzard bunch up like dat," Mary says.

"Nobody will bother 'em," Hazel says. *"Mess with dem bird and you go to jail."*

"Hush yuh mout, Hazel! Wuh fuh?"

"Buzzards keep the Market from bein' more stink up than it already is," Hazel says with a laugh. *"Dem workin' bird!"*

"Well, I ent gone get off dis train if dey workin' or not. I ready to go."

The doors close and the trolley rolls up Meeting Street and stops at Chapel Street.

 # CHAPTER 53

" **H** *ey eberybody,"* Peter says when he gets home from work.

"Hey husband," Mamie says from the kitchen.

"Dat smell good," he says and kisses her on the cheek. *"Wey yah get dem fush?"*

"Jacob ketch 'em," she says as her nephew sits at the table smiling proudly.

"Ooman, stop yuh lie," Peter say. *"Ent no fush dat big on Edisto."*

"I ketch 'em in dat creek yah tell me 'bout," Jacob says.

"Is you sho' 'bout dat?" Peter asks. *"I go git de Bible on yah."*

"Go 'head Uncle Peter, spin dat Bible on me ... I put muh han' on 'um an' say same ting: I ketch dem fush."

Peter reaches over and rubs Jacob's head.

"Weh yah Bible at," Jacob says and stands up. *"I git 'um fuh yah!"*

"Das OK, nephew, I b'leeb yah. Huh yuh catch 'em?"

"I ent kno 'xactly. I use cut mullet fuh bait."

CHAPTER 54

It's dark now on Chapel Street, Mary relaxes in the livingroom rocking chair smoking her new pipe and Hazel is working on invoices. They hear someone on the porch and the door opens.

"How ya'll doin?" Leon Jr. asks.

"We hungry. Let's eat." Hazel says.

"OK," Leon says. *"How Anna today?"*

"Anna better but the doctor says she'll be in the hospital in there a while longer," Hazel says. Mary quietly puffs on her pipe.

"Momma, you OK?" Leon asks.

"Anna ent look good son."

Leon walks over and kisses her forehead. *"Dr. Johnson say she go be OK, ent dat right?"*

Mary responds with another puff.

"Try not to worry, Momma. Dis yah las' night in Chass'tun. Mr. Sammy go be waitin' t'morruh fuh teke yah home."

She nods her head and forces a smile.

"He be at de landing at noon," Leon says as he pulls up a chair next to his mother. *"I wannuh see yah smile be' fo' yah leebe. Anna go be fine."*

"I OK son. Me an' Hazel hab a long day. I jis' tired."

Leon smiles. *"Is yah ready to moobe to Chass'tun now?"*

"No suh, I ent. Chass'tun too big. I ready to go home."

"Das wuh I thought."

Hazel gets up from the table and puts away her paperwork. *"I got some okra soup on the stove an' cornbread in the oven ... let's eat!"*

Mary and Leon sit at the table and Hazel gives each of them a bowl.

"Hazel," Mary says, *"I tas'e a lotta okra soup in all muh year in dis worl', an' dis wey up dey wid de bes'."*

"Thank yah Miss Mary. Glad yah like it. Taste the sausage?"

"I sho' do," Mary says and smiles, finally. Everyone finishes eating, Hazel clears the table and washes the dishes. *"I'm tired,"* she says as she dries her hands. *"Ya'll stay up and talk. I'm goin' to bed."*

Mary returns to the rocker and repacks her pipe. *"When I fus' get in dat hospital an' see Anna in dat rollin' chair, I 'mos' fall on de floor. Tank goodness Hazel stand'n' side me. She grab hol' muh hand an' keep me up... I nebuh see Anna look dat bad — all slump like dat. I look close while de nurse roll Anna to de winduh. Anna smile when her see me ... dat calm me down. Uh-huh."*

Leon takes his mother's hand. *"Same ting happ'n when I fus' see Anna in dat room."*

"I glad Dr. Johnson wuh dere," Mary says. *"Him tell me wuh wrong wid Anna, like 'e did 'bout yuh daddy, and tank Gawd fuh dat."*

"Das righ', Momma, das wuh yuh do when trouble come. I try to do dat eberyday ..."

# CHAPTER 55

It's early the next morning and Leon has already left. Hazel and Mary drink coffee and talk. The more Mary gets to know her daughter-in-law, the better she likes her.

"Dat sho' was good, Hazel. I ent kno' yah such a good cook, an' happy yah teke good care of Leon Jr. wid eberyting."

"Thank yuh, Miss Mary, I'm happy yah feel that way about me. I'm sad Anna got sick, but I'm glad we are spending time together ... Leon will be back directly. He left early to deliver fish. He didn't want to awaken yuh."

"Him ent wake me," Mary says with a smile. *"I hey 'um leebe. I git up ebery morn'n' b'fo' crack-uh-day."*

Hazel laughs. *"No way I can do that."*

"Hazel," Mary says, *"das good t'ick-cut bacon yah fix dis mornin'. Yah fry 'em up de weh I like 'um. An' yuh biscuit jis' right too."*

"The bacon is from the Market. The man cuts it as thick as you want. I've wrapped some for you to take to Wadmalaw."

"Tank yuh honey. Yah a good 'ooman, Hazel. I glad yuh marry muh son. When yuh do ting from de heart like yah do, de Lawd bless yuh. No, b'fo' I leebe, I ax fuh a big fabuh?"

"What yah need Miss Mary?"

Mary, whose eyes are tearing up, says, *"Please go see Anna when yah can. I kno' dat Leon Jr. try, but 'e work ha'd all day mos' eberyday, an' 'e ent kno' much 'bout dat 'sumption. So do dat fuh me."*

"I'll do that every day, Miss Mary, so don' worry 'bout it."

"Tank yuh, Hazel."

"Miss Mary," Hazel says as she reaches over and takes her mother-in-law's hand. *"There's a reason I haven't come with Leon to see yah at Wadmalaw… I'm afraid of all that water between here and there. I'm afraid of water because somethin' bad happened when I was a child."*

"Wuh dat, Hazel?"

"I was raised up the highway between Sandy Island and Georgetown, and I … I …"

Hazel has tried hard to forget the day when the boat turned over and her mother and siblings drowned. She tries to tell Mary more but the words don't come.

"Honey," Mary says, *when bad ting happen, turn 'um obuh to de Lawd. He go work 'um out fuh yah. Dat Gawd's promise, an' Gawd ent lie!"*

Tears well up in Hazel's eyes as the women hear Leon out on the porch. Hazel reaches in her dress pocket, removes a handkerchief and dries her tears.

"Hey Momma, Mr. Sammy go be dere waitin' at noon. Yah ready?"

"Eberyting all pack up, son. I ready when you is."

"Good. Hazel, Mr. Goldberg go be by later wid some money."

Hazel says nothing.

"Wuh wrong, Honey?"

"I'm OK. Miss Mary and I been talking …

Leon says nothing.

"I tell yah de trute, Leon," Mary says as they walk down East Bay Street to the Market landing. *"I usetuh tink Hazel uppity, buh I kno' her ent like dat now."*

"Tank yuh, Momma. Hazel a good 'ooman who ent got nobody to talk wid 'cept me. A 'ooman need a 'ooman fuh talk to. Hazel glad yah come."

They arrive at the landing and see Mr. Sammy and Joe waiting at the dock. Mary's heart beats faster as she walks to the boat. It's a long ride back to Wadmalaw and she's nervous, but not as nervous as Hazel would be, Mary says to herself.

CHAPTER 56

*O*K, *Mr. Big Fush Jacob,"* Peter tells his nephew. *"Bring dem two pine plank to me."* Jacob is busy helping his uncle build a coffin for a family who lives nearby. The deceased is Mr. Nathan Green, but most folks call him "Nubby" because he wrestled alligators when he was young. Nubby was only five feet tall. He'd wade out into the swamp, grab a six-foot gator by the head, slip a rope around the snout and drag the thing to shore. He would kill the gator by slitting its throat, and sold the meat and skin. Only once did the rope break, which cost him two fingers. He never set foot in the swamp since then.

Nubby, 78, had been sick for a while — for so long, in fact, that folks forgot he got sick in the first place. His heart stopped during a Sunday church service, which took the congregation by surprise. He was a founder of Edisto Island's Missionary Baptist Church and well known as an excellent teller of tall tales, ghost stories mostly. He was short in stature but long on talking. His casket was so small that Jacob thought Nubby was a child.

"Ent go hab nuttin' to do wid dat," he told Peter. *"Ent go mek no box fuh bury no chil'."*

His uncle quickly set the boy straight. *"I nebuh meke no coffin fuh no chillum befo', and I ent go sta't now. Mr. James mek 'um fuh all de young'un wuh pass. Him say dat worry him some but ent nobody else can do it."*

Jacob and Peter finished the job and Mr. James took the boy back to Wadmalaw the next day.

CHAPTER 57

*M*r. Sammy, Joe and Mary arrived by boat after a day long trip on from Charleston. Mr. James, who was waiting with his horse and wagon. He tied Jimey's reins to a tree branch and hurried down to help Mary get out of the boat. As James walked her up to the wagon, Sammy and Joe secured the boat then grabbed Mary's bags.

"Sistuh Mary," Mr. Sammy says. *"Hope de trip back bin OK."*

"I fine, Brudduh Sammy. Tank yah!"

"Sammy de Cap'n; I jis de crew," Joe says with a laugh as he puts her bags in the wagon.

Mr. Sammy tells James, *"OK, ol' man. I got Miss Mary 'cross de watuh, now yah get 'um to de house."*

"Hey Sammy," James responds. *"Muh daddy say when him be lil', yah sho' 'um huh to fush. Dat mean you de ol' man round hey now."*

"Hol' on, hol' on James … I ent grow up wid yah daddy," Sammy says, then turns to Mary and adds, *"James lie from de time 'e wake up til de time him go to bed!"*

James turns the horse and wagon around and everyone, still laughing, share goodbyes. Joe and Sammy head back to the boat for their trip across the creek to Johns Island.

When James and Mary are on the road to her house, he says, *"Ol' man Sammy kno' dat water… him sho' do."*

"Dat fuh true, tank de Lawd," she says.

James tells Mary that he fed the chickens as he promised, adding, *"Ent much mo' happ'n round hey while yah gone … Huh Anna doin'?"*

"Anna bery sick wid de 'sumption. She lock up in a big room in dat hospital wid oduh sick folk."

James remains quiet.

"At fus', I ent know wuh to tink. Buh Dr. Johnson say 'e tink her go be alright aftuh while."

"All us kin do now is pray," James says.

"Das de trute Brudduh James, uh-huh."

It's almost dark and Jacob is waiting on the porch for Mary to return. He hears something on the road and sees Jimey pulling the wagon. Jacob runs across the front yard and greets them.

"Hello Jacob," Mr. James says, *"Hey us is!"*

Mary says nothing, quietly relieved that she's home.

The next afternoon Jacob ran down to the landing to greet Leon Jr. When Jacob reached Mr. Sammy's boat, he could see in his uncle's eyes that something was wrong. Leon said very little as they walked to Mary's house, where she was waiting on the porch.

A few days earlier, Jacob was out walking in the woods when a strange mist enveloped him. Then, from behind a large hickory tree, out steps a man. Jacob narrows his focus:

"*Granddaddy, dat you?*"

"*Afternoon, Jacob.*" Big Leon's voice was rich and clear. His message was not. "*Jacob, trouble comin' an' yah mus' face 'um like a man.*"

"*Wuh dat?*" Jacob asked.

"*Yah Momma gwine to de Lawd t'night,*" Big Leon said.

Jacob was stunned but only a single tear rolled down his cheek. "*Huccome Gawd teke Momma aftuh her bin feelin' bettuh?*"

Big Leon slipped behind the big tree and stepped out on the other side. "*Don' ax why Gawd do wuh Him do.*" He stepped back behind the tree again and said nothing.

Jacob walked over to the tree and looked all round. Big Leon was gone.

Meanwhile, Mary was inside her house sitting near the fire and thinking about Anna. That's when she heard someone at the door.

"*Jacob, dat you?*"

"*No, Momma, it me.*"

Mary opened the door and saw her oldest son. "*Wuh wrong, Leon?*"

Tears welled up in Leon's eyes. "*Anna dead, Momma.*"

Not long after that Jacob arrived and saw his uncle and grandmother sitting at the table. "*Wuh up Uncle Leon?*"

Leon looked at his mother then turned to Jacob:

"*The doctuh told me dis mornin' dat yah momma run a febuh again an' hab trouble breathin', buh I already kno' sump'n ent right. Yesterday, Hazel an' me at de hospital an' Anna ax 'bout eberybody, and say she luv all ob we. Den her say, 'Leon, bring Jacob to de city to lib wid Hazel an' you. OK?*"

Jacob steps back and stares out into the darkness. The wind picks up slightly and he turns back around.

Leon continues:

On de way home Hazel say she worried ... Next day at the hospital de nurse tell us to wait in an empty room. Aftuh while, Dr. Johnson come in, place 'e hand on muh shouduh an' say, 'Anna pass.'"

Jacob listened a while longer, then went to bed.

CHAPTER 58

Leon Jr. left early the next morning for Charleston to arrange the return of his sister's remains to Wadmalaw. He had already asked Mr. Sammy to meet him at the landing. The next afternoon, Leon Jr. and Sammy returned to the landing in two boats, one of which carried a casket that held Anna's body. Meanwhile, word spread fast that Anna's wake would be the following night, and the funeral would be the day after that.

On the day before the funeral, Mr. Sammy and Mr. James told Mary they would spend the night inside the church and watch over the casket, as was customary. As they were about to leave Mary's house, Jacob said:

"Nana, I go stay wid Momma t'night too."

"Huccome?" she asked.

"Go mek sho' Momma alrigh'," he said, which took Mary by surprise. Sitting up all night with the casket was man's work. But she knew Jacob was determined, so she said OK.

It's dark now in the church and Jacob stretches out on a bench near the casket, which is in front of the altar. His uncles settle on the floor on the other side of the building near the front door, where a steady breeze keeps them cool. Jacob slept and dreamed. He rose early the next morning, quietly bid his uncles goodbye and left for his grandmother's house. As he walked in the early morning light, he reflected on a dream he had the night before:

"Daddy, Daddy… lemme touch Jacob one more time," he heard a woman say in the darkness of the sanctuary.

"No, Anna, us mus' go now," a man said. *"Jacob go see yah soon, I promise."*

Jacob recognized his grandfather's voice, tried to open his eyes, but couldn't. The sweet smell of honeysuckle filled the sanctuary, and Jacob was at peace. He awoke at daybreak and left. As he walked back to his grandmother's house a warm wind whistled through the long-leaf pines and rustled the thick palmetto fronds. Jacob stopped, listened:

"Be skrong, Jacob… Yah mus' be skrong."

"Das you?" the boy asked.

⚫ CHAPTER 59

B y the time the funeral processional entered the front doors of the island church, the sun was high and glistened through the stained-glass window behind the altar. It was 11:45 a.m. and the sanctuary was full. People stood in the back and others gathered outside, listening as best they could to what was happening inside. Mary sat with her immediate family on the front row closest to the casket. *"Lawd, Lawd, Lawd. Wuh I go do now… Anna gone an' I ent kno' 'xactly why. I weak now, Lawd. Gib me skrengt'. He'p me Jedus. Come to me Holy Ghos'…"*

The Rev. James Daniels officiated. He had known Anna since they were children on Wadmalaw. Dr. Johnson and one of Anna's nurses were there too. They sat behind Mary alongside Mr. Fleming's oldest son and two of Big Leon's aunts. Jacob sat between Emma and his grandmother, his eyes fixed on the casket and thinking about Big Leon's words in the wind.

The Rev. Daniels rises from his chair, looks down at Mary and says:

"Anna done sta't her journey, uh-huh … Her on de road to where dey ent no sickness, ent' no pain, ent no worry and no mo' pain …" He lifts his head up, spreads his arms, raises his voice and declares: *"Sistuh Anna goin' to be wid de Lawd. Oh, yeah! Uh-huh! I see 'um now, all dress in white, walkin' up de road to Paradise! Uh-huh, Uh-huh! … Now I see her standin' at de gate of pearls, an' I hea' de angels singin':*

'Holy, holy, holy … Lawd Gawd A'mighty!
Holy, holy, holy! Lord God A'mighty!
Early in de mo'ning our song rise to Thee;
Holy, holy, holy! Merciful and mighty!
God in three Person, bless'ed Trinity!

The pastor looks back down at Mary, smiles and looks up again:

I see Jedus standin' dere … 'e waitin' wid 'e arm open, uh-huh! I see Anna drop on she knee befo' Him, an' 'e say, "Welcome, chil' … Welcome home!"

Several members of the congregation jump to their feet and shout, *"Tank yah Lawd! Hab mercy, Gawd, hab mercy! Oh, muh Jedus, too! Tank yah, tank yah, tank yah!"*

And the preacher preached, and the people sang, and even Jacob joined in the chorus. After more than an hour of preaching and singing and shouting, Charlotte is overcome with emotion and faints. Two ushers hurry over, help her up and walk her out the front door. Mary sits down and prays a silent prayer while Cousin Emma burst into tears and Jacob wraps his arm around her.

Jacob, in fact, is the only member of the family who remains calm. He wants to tell his grandmother about his dream night before, but remains silent. When the service ends, Jacob stands near the front door as the pallbearers carry out the coffin. Everyone except for Aunt Mamie, who is pregnant, follows them out back to the burial site. Mamie knows that a pregnant woman in the graveyard during the burial ceremony is bad luck, so she waits on the church steps.

After a while Pastor Daniels concludes his graveside comments with reference to ashes and dust, he reaches down, grabbs a handful of dirt and sprinkles it on the coffin. The only child of the family under the age of twelve is little Sarah. Peter picks her up and carefully passes her over Anna's casket to Benjamin, who takes the child in his arms and walks through the crowd back to the church. Charlotte, who has composed herself, follows them closely. Everyone knows the "passing over" ensures that loved ones would never forget Anna's face. The mourners soon disperse while three men remove their jackets, pick up shovels and finish the burial.

"You ready to go?" Emma asks Jacob, both of whom remain near the grave and watch as the men place a coffee cup, a tin plate, a spoon, a fork and a small sewing kit — all from Mary's house — on top of the grave. These items will be of use to Anna in the afterlife, Leon Jr. had explained earlier to Jacob. Emma leaves for Mary's house. Jacob opts to stay.

Moments later he reaches into his pocket and removes a vial of crumbled honeysuckle flowers. *"Momma, dis fuh you,"* he says as he carefully places the jar atop the fresh dirt. He reaches back into his pocket, grabs the button his grandfather gave him and holds it to his right eye. He narrows his focus through the tiny hole in the button's face and searches above and around the grave. He sees nothing unusual, wipes away sweat from his brow and smiles again. The sky is blue and full of beautiful white clouds — a sure sign his mother is in heaven.

By the time Jacob gets back to the house, Mary, her sons, Emma and the others have changed clothes and sit around the table eating and talking.

"Jacob, git sump'n to eat," his grandmother says.

"I ent hungry, Nana." Jacob steps out onto the porch then sits in the rocker. Mary had hoped he would tell everyone what was on his mind.

Three weeks later Mary is still waiting for that conversation. Jacob has returned to work with Mr. James and Emma is on the boat to Savannah. Before she left she told Jacob: *"I will think of you every day. I promise."*

Months later, all is quiet on Wadmalaw Island. Jacob thinks he hears spirit voices in the breeze when walking down to Rouse's Creek. But he is not sure if they are voices or merely the wind.

Late one afternoon just before sunset, extremely dark clouds roll in from the west, and everything is strangely quiet except for an odd crackling sound in the woods. In the distance, Jacob hears a roar, which gets louder and louder. A sudden wind kicks up, bending the tall pines almost sideways. Moss is blown from the limbs of the live oaks. Jacob drops to his knees and crawls into a shallow ditch beside the road.

That's when a rogue tornado touches down, twisting and churning and snapping pines like toothpicks. Jacob gets as close to the ground as he can. Dirt, sand, leaves, limbs and other debris sweep across the road. Jacob covers his head and ears to protect himself and block out the incredibly loud noise. Minutes later, the twister lifts up and away. Jacob slowly stands up and looks around. The twister's path of destruction is wide and shocking. He runs a mile or so back to the house to check on his grandmother. As he reaches the front yard he sees trees are down but the house is still standing.

"Nana, Nana, is you OK?" he yells.

Jacob hears nothing until he gets to the porch.

"Nana, is you inside?"

"I OK, Jacob, but de roof leak' again. Tank Gawd dat storm gone and I see yah standing dey!"

Two days later Leon Jr., Benjamin and Peter are at the house. They have rounded up some materials to patch the leaks. Mary has moved in with Mamie and Peter while work on the roof is under way.

"Dat should do fuh now but Momma house need a tin roof," Leon Jr. tells Peter and Benjamin, both of whom agree. *"I gwine back to Chass'tun in de*

mornin' cause I hea' de fush callin' muh name. I be back aftuh fall fushin' ober. I go bring wood, nail an' tin, an' we put de new roof on 'um."

Peter and Benjamin agree, and gather up their tools. Leon Jr. tells Jacob to stick around for a while. *"I got sometin' to ax yah."*

"Wuh dat?" Jacob asks.

"Well, Jacob, aftuh us get dat new roof on Nana house, I wanna teke yah to Chass'tun to lib wid Hazel and me."

CHAPTER 60

It's was a beautiful day in late November when Leon returned to Wadmalaw with a boatload of wood and tin, and work on the new roof began early the next day. Leon, Peter, Benjamin and Jacob completed the job in two days. Mary returned that afternoon from Edisto. Jacob and Leon Jr. wasted no time packing for the trip to Charleston.

"Well, Momma, we set. Go leeb in de mornin'," Leon says. *"I bring Jacob back soon to see yuh. If 'e don' wanna go back to Chass'tun, 'e ent hab to."*

Mary wipes a tear from her eye and says, *"I OK wid dat son. Dis good fuh Jacob, buh I go be sad when ya'll go. I go miss habin' dat boy — who almos' a man now."*

Jacob says nothing.

A couple of hours later Jacob and his uncle are in the boat in the middle of Wadmalaw Sound. Leon locks down the oars and says, *"OK, show me wuh Mr. James teach yah about runnin' wid rudduh an' sail."*

Jacob wastes no time trading seats. Leon unties the sail and hands the line to his nephew, who grabs the rudder with his right hand and the rope with the other. A steady breeze fills the sheet and off they go across the sound.

"Mr. James be right … yah kno' wuh yah doin'," Leon says.

Jacob and his uncle take turns sailing and rowing to Charleston, but don't say much along the way.

"Jacob, if yah wanna tell me wuh on yah mind, I list'n'," Leon said when they reached the Stono River.

"Well, I tinkin' 'bout Emma … "

"I unduhstand," his uncle said. *"Ent nutt'n go stay de same. Yah ent got to say no mo' 'bout dat unless yah wanna."*

Jacob had plenty of time to think about a lot of things that day: Emma, his grandmother, island life and the visits by Big Leon.

"You ent go forget me is yah, Cuz?" he remembered Emma asking before she left. *"I ent go fuhget,"* he says to himself repeatedly.

"I go miss habin' dat boy — who almos' a man now," he remembered his grandmother saying. He also recalls Big Leon's warning about being strong.

After the boat passed through Elliott's Cut and reached the Ashley River, Jacob broke the silence: *"Sho' am big, Uncle Leon,"* he says when he sees Charleston for the first time.

Leon smiles. *"De water fast an' smooth through hey, but go be chop up when us cross de Ashley. So hold on."*

Sure enough, as the boat sails into the river's outflow, the water surface gets rough. When they reach the Charleston Battery, Jacob mans the oars. His arms ache with each pull alongside the city wall to the mouth of the Cooper River on the eastern side of the peninsula. A steady wind kicks up and Leon releases the sail again. They glide past the wharves to the Market landing.

Jacob is well prepared for living in Charleston. When Anna was sick, Leon promised Mary that, if Jacob's mother did not recover, he and Hazel would raise him like a son. When he explained this to his nephew, Jacob readily accepted the offer, having long dreamed of moving to Charleston to be with his mother. He is convinced that he will see and talk to Anna's spirit there from time to time.

Jacob and Leon land the wide wooden craft, unload their gear, secure the boat and walk up to Chapel Street.

"Hey Jacob, welcome... I got dinnuh fuh yah," says Hazel, standing in the doorway.

"I hongry, Auntie." Jacob already feels like he's home.

 CHAPTER 61

Weeks later, Jacob is in the yard storing Uncle Leon's nets in the large wooden box. As he works, he thinks about Aunt Hazel, who in certain ways reminded him of his mother, especially the softness of her voice. They have talked a lot together, and he has noticed she sometimes gets lost in thought like his mother used to do. Jacob finishes with the nets, closes the box and returns to the house, where Hazel sits quietly at the kitchen table.

"Need anyting Auntie?" Jacob asks.

"Uh-huh, I do. Please take the fuel can to Mr. Goldberg's store and get it filled with kerosene." She gives Jacob a quarter to cover the purchase, and soon, with container in hand, he is out the door.

Jacob likes talking to Mr. Goldberg, although the old man is hard of hearing. Jacob has to speak loudly, which he seldom does normally. Uncle Leon had introduced him to Mr. Goldberg soon after Jacob arrived in Charleston. Jacob also enjoys delivering fresh seafood to the store and being paid for services rendered.

"Mornin' Mr. Goldberg!" Jacob shouts as he enters the store.

"Mornin' Jacob," he says as he shuffles to the front counter. *"You here early, young man. What you got for me today?"*

"I hey fuh kerosene," Jacob shouts as he hands Mr. Goldberg the fuel can.

"Oh, OK," he replies. He takes the empty container back to where he keeps fuel in a large metal tank with hand pumps. As Jacob waits, he eyes the multitude of items in glass jars with colorful labels lining the shelves behind the counter. He focuses on a small can of tobacco and is reminded of his grandmother.

"Here you go Jacob," Mr. Goldberg says as he returns. *"That'll be a quarter."*

Jacob hands him the money. *"I be back dis aftuhnoon wid some fush, Mr. Goldberg,"* he yells as he leaves.

"Put dat kerosene on de po'ch fuh now, Jacob," Hazel says when he returns.

"Yes ma'am."

"I need mo' wood for cookin'," she says.

"Alrigh', Auntie I git 'um now."

When Jacob first came to live on Chapel Street, he was very quiet, didn't eat much and often sat mesmerized by the flames in the fireplace. Leon Jr. told Hazel about his nephew's odd ways, including the fact that he was born with the veil and had the birthmark. Hazel remembered how stoic Jacob was when she told him about Anna's final days at the hospital.

Jacob returns to the house. *"Dis go be enuf?"* he asks.

"Oh yeah. Tank yah!"

It has not taken Jacob long to learn his way around the streets and alleys of Charleston. Growing up on the island, there were no road signs so he developed a good sense of direction. In Charleston, he follows the trolley tracks whenever he isn't sure how to get back to the house. Leon told him the tracks would eventually reach Meeting and Chapel streets. Jacob prefers to walk because he wants to learn as much as he can about the neighborhoods in case Mr. Goldberg asks him to deliver seafood somewhere.

"Mornin'," Jacob says now as he passes folks on the sidewalks. Some return his greeting, but others, mostly white folks, do not as if he isn't there. Leon and Hazel forewarned him about this, saying city folks generally are not as friendly as those who live on the island.

Jacob stays busy helping his uncle and aunt since arriving in Charleston. He has also met the fishermen who work with his uncle. He proudly told the men about being the first mate for Mr. James, and that they fished, shrimped and dug oysters in the rivers and creeks around Wadmalaw. He enjoys hearing Leon Jr. brag to the crew about his nephew's reputation with a cane pole, a hook and piece of mullet.

Jacob was spellbound the first time he visited the city Market. He had never seen or smelled so much seafood, vegetables and meats for sale to so many people. He marveled at the cuts of hogs, chickens and lamb for sale, as well as all the shrimp, fish, crabs, sharks, oysters, scallops, clams and stingrays purchased there day after day.

Jacob and his uncle often walk through the Market in route to the fleet's boats at the Cooper River landing. He looks forward to going out to sea with the fleet someday. He has also met dockworkers who knew his grandfather. Soon they called Jacob "Little Big Fish" in Leon Sr.'s honor. He also befriended several boys who live on Charleston's Eastside. They include two chimney sweeps. He has never seen them when they are not covered in soot. They are much smaller that Jacob, and their hair is cut very short. They told Jacob about climbing onto rooftops and lowering themselves into chimneys where they use sticks with rags tied on the ends to scrub burnt resins off the bricks inside the chimneys.

Jacob always knew when he was close to the Market. He could smell it. Most of the fish and meats are cleaned and cut behind the stalls and the leftovers are tossed into the street for the buzzards. The stench is especially severe on hot days — and there are many in Charleston.

But on this fall day Jacob did not walk all the way to the Market. It was cool at 11:30 a.m. when he reached Calhoun Street, so he turned left and went to Gadsden's Wharf, one of several docks on the Cooper River where for years ships' cargoes have been loaded and unloaded. Jacob walks along the wharf and stares across the harbor to the Atlantic Ocean.

Various transactions occur on Gadsden Wharf between fishermen and the fishmongers who sell seafood in Charleston. The locals gather here to catch up on the latest gossip. They say it was on this wharf where thousands of enslaved Africans were removed from the holds of trans-Atlantic sailing ships in which they were chained for months during the Middle Passage from their West African homelands to the New World.

One story especially troublesome for Jacob is about 66 enslaved men, women and children who were left chained together on the wharf inside a huge iron cage for the night. The ship's captain, who was behind schedule, had arranged for his human cargo to be auctioned off early the next day. But the man hired to watch over the cage got drunk that night and passed out. It was a full moon, clouds rolled in from the east, the tide was exceptionally high and a sudden storm blew in off the ocean. The next morning the huge cage was in the water between the wharf and the shore. Inside were the bodies of 47 men, 13 women and six children. They had managed to break open some bars but could not free themselves of their heavy chains.

The fisherman who shared the story told Jacob that on nights when the moon is full and the wind is blowing from the northeast, he has heard screams and moans and the clanging of chains against the bars.

 CHAPTER 62

A few days later, a dozen or so fishermen are on Gadsden's wharf when Jacob arrives. They were gathered around an exceptionally large man with black, braided hair streaked with gray. He wears a union jacket and red cotton gloves, the fingers of which have been removed. His braid dangles between his shoulders. He carries a heavy walking stick — black with a silver snakehead handle brightly shined. A large silver ring is on the fourth finger of his right hand, and his eyes flash fiery red as if extremely irritated.

"Aftuhnoon," Jacob says as he approaches the group. No one says anything to Jacob. All attention is focused on the angry, red-eyed man. After a while,

Mr. Rhett, one of the onlookers, whispers to Jacob, *"Don't say nutt'n boy."*

The man with the snakehead stick finishes talking, and the crowd quickly disperses.

"Dat man dey, 'e a damn fool," Mr. Rhett whispers. *"Him bettuh not mess wid me t'day."*

"Who dat man?" Jacob asks.

"Dat Constable Red Eye, buh don' let 'um hey yah say dat. Red Eye ent like to hea' his nickname, an' 'e mean as a snake. Red Eye carry dat cane cause 'e 'pose to be a police officer, buh him crooked as a copperhead, and ent fraid to strike yah wid dat stick.

Red Eye is one of several men the city has hired as so-called constables, whose authority is limited to black folk only. Landlords pay him on the side to collect rent from tenants along the waterfront. He never gives a receipt and keeps some of what he collects. When tenants get behind on their bills, he threatens them with eviction or arrest or both unless they pay whatever he demands.

"Buh dat ent all," Mr. Rhett continues. *"If de tenant a good-lookin' gal, Red Eye meke special 'rangement, if yah kno' wuh I mean. Red Eye also kno' how to use de root. Red Eye a conjureman … 'e kno' hoodoo and all like dat."*

Mr. Rhett points at Red Eye's right hand. *"Dat ring got power. Red Eye use 'um to cast spell dat meke yah sick. An' 'e kno' how to mix up a po'tion dat meke yah feel bettuh. Dey say 'e meke a hot day cold, a wet day dry, a good day bad and a bad day good. Das wuh dey say 'bout Constable Red Eye."*

Jacob had heard about a conjureman while growing up on Wadmalaw — that he could calm storms and reverse unfavorable winds, and cast spells on folks for a fee. But Jacob had never seen a root doctor until now.

⦿ CHAPTER 63

"A ftuhnoon Uncle Leon; huh yah doin' Mr. Bobo," Jacob says when he arrives at the landing. Mr. Bobo is one of the fleet fishermen.

"Hey dey, nephew," Leon says. *Yah jis' in time to he'p us unload. Grab one dem basket fuh me."*

"Teke dis basket right hey fust," Mr. Bobo says smiling broadly. *"Dis too heaby fuh me!"*

That's when Mr. Smitty chimes in, *"No, boy, don' grab dat basket cause yah might strain yuhself . . . Yah nebuh go hab no chillum if yah do dat. Teke muh basket, 'e ent so heaby."*

"Bobo, leave Jacob 'lone. You too Smitty," Leon Jr. says then looks at Jacob. *"Grab hol' de udduh end ob dis basket."* he tells Jacob.

Jacob enjoys listening to the men and doesn't mind helping them with the fish, which jump out the baskets and land in the water and on the ground as they are moved from the boats to the wharf. It takes Jacob and the others about an hour to unload and sort the catch.

Later that day Jacob made fish deliveries to three stores and four homes between the Market and Chapel streets. He finished around 4 p.m. and got back to the house soon afterward. When he reached the porch, he smelled bread baking inside.

"Hey Aunt Hazel, sho' smell good in hey," he says as he walks through the door.

Hazel, who is sitting at the kitchen table, says, *"Das drop biscuit yah smell in the oben."*

She gets up, opens the oven and removes a pan full of biscuits with golden, brown crusts. Jacob's face lights up.

"Take one," Hazel says, *"but don' eat 'um yet. I get butter for yah."*

"No, Auntie, ent go wait fuh budduh," he says as he puts a whole biscuit in his mouth. *"Yum, das good."*

# CHAPTER 64

Mary's house has a new roof and she is living alone for the first time in her life. Earlier, she took a meal to her ailing neighbor, knowing the importance getting out, helping others and socializing. It's almost dark now and she sits on the porch. She packs her pipe and lights up.

Mary stayed on Edisto Island longer than planned to help Mamie following the birth of Peter Jr. She looks forward to returning soon for the child's naming ceremony, and is happy Peter and Mamie are continuing the tradition.

"Some tings don' change, tank Gawd," she says between puffs. Mary has talked to herself a lot since her grandson left the island. *"Wonduh huh my lil' Jacob doin','"* she whispers. *"I should say, wonduh huh my big Jacob doin' now."*

Indeed, Jacob is doing fine in Charleston. He enjoys fishing off wharves along the Cooper River, and trades his catch with street vendors for meats, vegetables and other items. Hazel likes that.

One of the vendors, Miss Lydia, sells deviled crabs and sweet potato pies on the streets. She reminds Jacob of his grandmother. He trades with her in the afternoon before leaving for home. *"Jacob, bring some mo' fush. I meke yah a good deal,"* she says every time she sees him.

Late one afternoon Jacob was fishing from a small dock not far from Chapel Street. He sat down, dangled his feet over the Cooper River and stared into the water at nothing in particular. After a while, a man's face appeared near the surface. Jacob rubbed his eyes with the palms of his hands and looked down again. Then he heard Big Leon's voice. He looked again and, sure enough, his grandfather's face shimmered in the water.

"Jacob, Jacob. Dis me."

"Wuh… wuh yah doin' down dey?"

"Come close so I kin see yah bettuh."

Jacob laid on his stomach and leaned as close to the water as he could. And there was Big Leon. His lips moved and words bubbled to the surface:

"I got sometin' to tell yah … listen carefully."

Jacob raised his head and looked all around to see if anyone was watching.

"Stop lookin' round, boy… Ent nobody comin'. Even if dey do, dey ent go see me."

"OK," Jacob says.

"Is yah listnin' carefully?"

"Yes sir."

"Yah momma go contact yah soon."

"Uh-huh."

"Now Jacob, 'membuh dat button I give yah?"

"Yes sir."

"Still got 'um?"

"Yes sir."

"Good. Dat wuh yah need to contact folk in de spirrut worl'," Big Leon says.

"I done did dat," the boy says.

"I kno'. Das why I talkin' to yah now. Yah list'nin' good."

"I list'nin', Grandaddy."

"Yah momma go call on you soon, probably while yah sleepin'. But yah might be 'wake when her do, so be ready all de time…"

"*OK Grandaddy.*"

Big Leon also asked about the devil's backbone. "*Still got 'um?*"

"*Yes sir, I got 'um.*"

"*Dat special,*" his grandfather says, "*cause 'e can heal folk dat sick, an' teke away dey pain.*"

Big Leon asked Jacob to stop at the vacant lot next to his aunt and uncle's house and look for a bay laurel tree — "*dat de one wid bright green, jaggedy leaf an' red berry. Mek sho' it got de red berry, not black ones. Pull 'um off t'ree along wid fo'r ob dem leaf an' put 'em yah pocket. Dey gib yah good luck, an' money too. Yah go need 'em soon. Buh yah gotta beleeb' to make 'em work.*"

"*I go do dat Grandaddy. Dem leaf an' berry help sick folk feel bettuh?*"

"*Das right ... an' dey go bring yah money too, but yah gotta beleeb' or dey 'ent work.*"

"*Huh come de doctuh ent use 'em on Momma?*"

"*Das sump'tin else, Jacob ... De Lawd got plan fuh yah momma, but I ent got time to tell yah 'bout dat cause de tide goin' out.*"

"*OK,*" Jacob says.

Big Leon told Jacob not to tell anyone about their conversation, but it didn't matter. Folks would not believe him anyway. However, the boy did believe, and looked forward to talking to his grandfather again, and his mother too. What he didn't want was to hear from any bad spirits, like those under the fig tree.

"*All kind ob spirrut go call on yah Jacob. Das wuh happen when yah bo'n wid de veil an' dat birt'mark,*" Big Leon said.

"*Yes sir. Kin I ax yuh one mo' ting?*" That's when Big Leon's face disappeared. Jacob stood up and pinched his cheek to tell if he was dreaming, which he wasn't.

That afternoon Jacob stopped at the lot next to his uncle's house and spotted the bay laurel tree with red berries. He picked off four jagged leaves and some berries and slipped them into his shirt pocket. He liked their aroma. Reminded him of Wadmalaw. When he got back to the house Aunt Hazel asked if he had caught any fish.

"*No ma'am.*"

"*That's alright. I go fry chicken tonight,*" she says.

That night, after everyone had gone to bed, Jacob slid his hand under the mattress and removed what he calls his "magic box." He used his fingers to pry off the lid and placed the aromatic leaves and berries alongside the button and the devil's backbone. He closed the lid, put the box back under the mattress and slipped under fresh sheets that Hazel washed earlier that day and dried outside on the clothesline.

Sure enough, Jacob dreamed about his mother: Anna was visiting Nana on Wadmalaw and telling Mary what happened in the hospital when what seemed like a large wave washed over them. Jacob, who thought he was drowning, woke up. He was soaked in sweat.

CHAPTER 65

Weeks have passed since Jacob saw his grandfather's face in the water, but he remembered what Big Leon said about the bay leaves and berries, that they could bring good luck to its possessor if the person believed it would. He soon got a chance to find out. Jacob left the house early on Monday, headed to the Market and saw Miss Lydia sitting on a stump selling deviled crabs and fresh flowers from a huge sweetgrass basket.

"Mornin', Miss Lydia."

"Hey Jacob… ent see yuh lately."

"Busy deliberin' fush. How yah doin?"

She grimaces in pain. *"I wanna sho' yah sump'in',"* she says and rolls up her the right sleeve of her tattered sweater past her elbow. *"Look a dis,"* she says, pointing to nasty sores on her upper arm. *"I try to clean 'em up, buh ent do no good. I tink dey 'fected. Ent nebuh had nuttin' like dis b'fo'."*

Jacob takes a close look at her arm. *"Is yah bin to see a doctuh?"*

"Ent got no doctuh … Ent got money fuh dat."

Jacob says, *"I goin' back to de house an' get sump'in fuh yah."*

Jacob went straight to his bedroom, grabbed the tin from under his mattress and removed the devil's backbone and two bay leaves. He pinched off a piece of the backbone, slipped it along with the leaves into his back pocket, closed the lid, put the tin back under the mattress and left.

"Miss Lydia, I got dis fuh yah," Jacob says when he returns. He reaches into his back pocket and hands her the twig and a leaf.

"Wuh dis is?"

"Dis de Devil backbone an' some special bay leaf… Squeeze some oil out de tip ob the bone an' out de end ob the leaf and an' rub 'um on yah arm… mek

'um feel bettuh."

"Is yah sho' 'bout dat?"

"Yes ma'am. I be back nex' week to check on yah!"

Jacob wasn't sure about the healing quality of juices because he had not used them yet. But he believed what his late grandfather told him. The next week Jacob got up earlier than usual and hurried down to see Miss Lydia, who was sitting there holding her flower basket.

"Huh yah doin', Miss Lydia?"

She looks him in the eyes and a smile transforms her wrinkled lips. *"Jacob, when yah gimme dem root, I ent kno' if dey go work. But I beleeb wuh yah say an' try 'em, an' dem sore dry up quick."* She rolls up the sweater sleeve and shows him her arm. *"Tank yah fuh dis..."*

Jacob looks at where the sores used to be.

"Kin yah git mo'?" she asks.

"I tink so."

Word spread fast and soon the street vendors were praising Jacob. They called him "Dr. Feel Good." One night during dinner, his uncle asked him, *"Wuh dis I hey 'bout Dr. Feel Good?"*

"Wey yah hey dat?" Jacob asks.

"Down round de Market ... Miss Lydia tellin' eberybody yah gib her some root dat heal she arm quick."

"Ent kno' dey say dat 'bout me. I jis' gib Miss Lydia a piece ob wuh call de Devil Backbone and some bay leaf, tell her to squeeze out some oil and rub on she sore, an' her say 'e fix 'um good."

Hazel, who is listening, asks Jacob, *"How you know about such things?"*

Jacob remembered what his grandfather told him about keeping the secret. He also knew Hazel was aware of his birthmark and the veil. So he took a deep breath and told his aunt and uncle about talking to Big Leon whose face was in the water by the Cooper River dock.

Leon Jr. sat quietly and listened while Hazel cleaned the table. After a while, Leon asks, *"Jacob, when did yah talk to yah grandaddy?"*

"A while back," Jacob replies. *"I see 'um in a dream at fust, then later I see 'e face fuh real in the water under one dem dock weh I go fushin ... an' 'e talk to me fuh sho b'fo de tide go out. Den 'e gone."*

Hazel and Leon listen as Jacob describes Big Leon's face in the water, and what his grandfather had told him about the button, the Devil's Backbone and the bay leaves.

"Jacob, listen to me," Leon Jr. says. *"Be careful goin' round he'pin' sick folk like dat. I ent sayin' yah shouldn't he'p 'em, buh if Constable Red Eye hey 'bout dat, 'e ent go be happy. Dat man tricky, an' hateful too. No tellin' wuh 'e might do."*

"Alrigh'," Jacob says. He remembered seeing Red Eye on the docks but didn't tell his uncle and aunt.

# CHAPTER 66

A week later Leon Jr. heard on the street that Constable Red Eye had been asking about Jacob and Miss Lydia. When he got home he told Jacob, *"Remember, wuh I tell yah 'bout Red Eye. Stay wey from him, yah hey me?"*

"Uh huh. I 'member," Jacob replied.

Leon later told Hazel what he had heard and asked her not to say anything to anyone, including Jacob. Late that night after Leon and Jacob had gone to bed, Hazel was working on the ledger but couldn't concentrate on the numbers. She worried about her nephew, his use of root medicine and what Constable Red Eye might do to him. She could not stop thinking about Jacob and his dreams, and vaguely recalled her aunts, who lived up the coast near Georgetown, talking about people born with the veil. But she couldn't recall exactly what they said.

Another week passed and Jacob's delivery service was booming. Most customers wanted fresh seafood, although a few street vendors requested his medicine for various ailments. Late one warm evening just after dark, Jacob finished his deliveries and headed home. As he passed an old cemetery on Smith Street, a chill wind blew in all around him. He felt lightheaded and sat down near the entrance to the walled burial ground. That's when the familiar aroma of honeysuckle filled the air. His head cleared a little so he stood up and peered through the iron gates. He thought he saw something move among a row of weathered headstones near the back wall.

A breeze brushed his face, only this time it came from inside the graveyard, blew past him and into the street. Along with it, Jacob heard a faint, familiar voice: *"I glad yah stop by, son, yah hea' me?"*

Jacob looked around the cemetery, then up and down the street, but saw no one. The aroma of his mother's favorite flower permeated the damp air but he saw no honeysuckle blooms, not even a vine. As he was no longer feeling faint, he left for home.

In the weeks that followed, he walked almost every day from Chapel Street to Smith Street, turned left and stopped for a while at the cemetery gate. Each time he stopped, he took a deep breath and peered through the ironwork at the gravestones, especially those lining the back wall. But to no avail. He saw nothing. Heard nothing. And the only aroma was damp earth and mildew.

One evening while sitting with his Aunt Hazel at the kitchen table, Jacob told her about a recent dream in which she appeared.

"What was it about?"

"It 'bout a woman and three chillum in a sinking boat," Jacob said, *"an' somebody yell yuh name."*

"Somebody yell 'Hazel'?" she asked.

"Oh yeah, Auntie, somebody holler: 'Hazel! Hazel! ... Don' panic chil'. Take deep breath, turn on yah back, relax and try to float!'"

Hazel leaned forward, stared deeply into Jacob's eyes and asked, *"What happ'n nex'?"*

"Dey wuh screamin' fuh help and splashin' all round 'til a wave wash obuh 'em. Den all be quiet."

"What happ'n aftuh dat?"

"Well, Auntie, nex' ting I kno' I standin' in de mud by de river, an' one ob dem chillum in de boat float on she back nex' to me. I grab she hand, lif' her up to she feet, an' I look skrait in dat gal face, and look familiar. Den all wuh quiet. I ent see or hea' nobody else. No boat, no nutt'n'. Just dat little girl, standin' dey lookin' up at me."

Hazel's eyes were wide like fresh daisies. *"Wuh happ'n nex'?"*

"Well, de girl ax weh eberybody at? I say I ent kno'. De girl sta't cryin' an' callin' fuh her momma ... an' dat when I wake up."

Hazel was stunned but said nothing more about it that evening. It was no secret she was afraid of water, and well known that she was six years old on the water with her mother and two siblings when the boat turned over and everyone except Hazel drowned. What folks did not know was Hazel didn't panic. She rolled over on her back and floated to shore where a man — she does not know who — grabbed her hand and pulled her out, and she never saw him again.

Hazel had managed to put the details of that terrible day out of her mind until Jacob mentioned his dream.

"That chil' was me," she told her husband the next morning. *"That's why I'm afraid of water."*

"Huh could dat be?" Leon asked. *"Jacob ent born when dat happen."*

"I don't know," Hazel whispered.

 # CHAPTER 67

On Memorial Day in May 1917, Mary's family again gathered on Wadmalaw Island for festivities filled with joy, laughter and good food. Jacob's uncles, aunts and cousins were there as usual. Emma stopped by the house for a visit, and Jacob was glad to see her. They talked at great length about their lives in Savannah and Charleston. Even his Aunt Hazel was there.

For Hazel, the boat trip from Charleston was a challenge, but she appreciated having loved ones, especially Mary, to lean on when anxiety threatened her. One evening she was sitting with Mary on the porch and told her mother-in-law about the drownings and Jacob's dream.

"Uh-huh," Mary responded, adding, *"I tink Jacob go soon cross ober to de odduh side."*

"What yah mean?" Hazel asked.

"Well, I ent sayin' Jacob go die... I sayin' him cross ober ebery now an' den. Jacob got dat gif' and now 'e dreamin' like dem ol' folk wid de gif' did ... Great Gawd hab mussy!"

The next morning Mary took Jacob aside and said, *"Us ent talk yet like I wanna... buh dat go hab to wait 'til I see yuh again cause yah goin' back to Chass'tun soon."*

"Alrigh' Nana," he whispered, *"us talk later, buh I ent kno' when I be back."*

CHAPTER 68

It's late September in Charleston and Jacob has been throwing his cast net for shrimp in shallow areas on the west side of the Cooper River. He has had good luck in this area during the cooler fall months when the shrimp have matured in the salt creeks and head out to the ocean. Last year he sold several pounds of these creek shrimp to Mr. Goldberg at the corner store, and plans to catch even more this season. Before he left the house, his Uncle Leon said with a chuckle, *"I proud ob yah fuh workin' so ha'd, Jacob. Yah 'bout to run me outta bidness."*

"Ent no way I go do dat," Jacob smiled and said.

Indeed, Jacob was doing well, happy living with his uncle and aunt. But that afternoon Jacob and several men were fishing off a dock not far from the Market when Constable Red Eye, with snake-head stick in hand, walked straight to a slender man who often fished there. Everybody called the man Geronimo. Red Eye got in Geronimo's face and cut loose with a cussing like Jacob had never heard before. The boy didn't know what half the curse words meant, but knew the constable meant business.

"You a Gawd damn liar, Red Eye, get wey from me wid all dat!" Geronimo screamed.

Red Eye puffed himself up like an ugly toad fish, lifted his cane over his head and yelled: *"I ent go leeb yah 'lone 'til yah pay me. Nex' time I come round hey, yah bettuh hab dat damn money! Don' mek me haffa hurt yuh, understand?"*

The constable and the fisherman went back and forth like this for a while as everyone else on the dock gathered round them, watched and listened. Geronimo stood his ground, never even flinched, then gathered up his gear and hollered, *"I ent skay'd ob you, Red Eye. Go to Hell! Go skrait to Hell!"*

That's when Constable Red Eye drew back his big stick with the snake-head handle like he was going to pummel the man. *"Hell is muh second' home — boy — an' when I visit down dey nobody mess wid me,"* Red Eye hissed. *"I done beat de hell out de Devil hisself, and ent skay'd ob nuttin'. I go beat de hell out you too if yah ent got dat damn money when I see yuh again!"*

The constable did not strike Geronimo, but his eyes lit up like they were on fire, maybe even smoking a little, Jacob thought. Red Eye turned and yelled *"Git out my way!"* to the onlookers then stormed off dock. Moments later, Geronimo left in the opposite direction. That's when one of the men standing near Jacob said, *"Geronimo Watson got hisself a bad problem."*

Jacob had heard of a man named Geronimo who used to live on Wadmalaw, and recalled that the man had spent time in prison for killing his wife.

"Geronimo ent owe Red Eye nuttin'," another man said. *"Red Eye want eberybody to be skay'd ob him, buh 'e ent go 'timidate Geronimo. Geronimo ent skay'd ob nobody."*

CHAPTER 69

As Jacob was falling asleep that night a cool breeze blew in through an open window and after a while a female voice asked: *"Jacob, huhcome you ent stay an' talk to me?"*

"Momma, das you?" Jacob asked. The window curtains ruffled again and he heard her say:

"Jacob, I call yah from de grabe ya'd, buh you ent come to me."

"I ent know dat bin you, Momma. I ent see nobody."

"Ent you smell de honeysuckle?"

"Yes ma'am. I smell 'um. Wey you at now Momma?"

The curtains ruffled again, the scent was gone and all was silent.

The next day Jacob left the house early and headed to the Market. Storm clouds had formed in the Atlantic over the harbor jetties as he stopped at Gadsden's Wharf see if anybody was catching anything. Several men were there with their lines out and among them was Geronimo Watson.

One of the men introduced Jacob to Geronimo, who said, *"I hey 'bout yuh, Jacob. You from Wadmalaw, init? I got some people down dey frum Seabrook."*

"Uh-huh," Jacob replied.

"I kno' yuh Uncle Leon. Dey call 'um Little Fush an' 'e a good man," Geronimo continued.

"Yes sir. Das my uncle," Jacob said proudly.

Geronimo smiled broadly until his focus shifted to something behind the boy. Jacob turned around and saw Constable Red Eye with cane in hand walking up the wharf. Thunder growled in the distance and the wind picked up considerably from the northeast. Geronimo lifted his pants slightly, stood as tall as he could and said, *"Sorry, Jacob, I got bidness to do."*

Jacob stepped aside to make way for what seemed to be Satan himself, with the fingers of his right hand wrapped tight around the neck of the snake's head that adorned the top of his big, black cane. Red Eye stopped directly in front of Geronimo. The constable's eyes were as red as smoking hot coals that illuminated his entire face. His nose — pitted, crinkled and flared — was only an inch away from the top of Geronimo's head. Geronimo was short and thin but he stood his ground. A bolt of lightning struck somewhere in the vicinity of the Morris Island lighthouse followed seconds later by a double-clap of thunder.

"Gimme my damn money!" Red Eye roared, his breath rank like rotten eggs. Everyone on the dock picked up the stench and backed away from the combatants.

"I done tol' yah Red Eye: Go to hell, yuh son-ob-de-Debil's bitch," Geronimo yelled.

Dark clouds rolled in and whitecaps quickly roiled the river. Jacob and the others steadied themselves on the wobbly wharf.

"I ent skay'd ob yah … So, git out my Gawd damn face!" Geronimo said as he took two steps backward. Lightning lit the sky and a clap of thunder shook the pilings upon which the wooden wharf had stood for more than a century.

Red Eye looked up and Geronimo snatched a rusty ice pick from his leather belt. Red Eye looked back down, lifted his snake-head stick by its tail and screamed, *"Gimme dat money b' fo I strike yah dead."* With that, the rickety wharf shook violently and the snake-head cane commenced to rattling. Geronimo screamed *"Ya-e-yah"* as loud as he could, cocked his right arm and slammed the icepick into the constable's massive chest.

Red Eye dropped his cane, clutched his bloodied chest with both hands and turned as if to leave. But he didn't go anywhere — except to his knees. The ice pick had found its mark. With a punctured heart Red Eye collapsed with a thud on the dock as blood spewed from the hole in his chest like stinking hot lava from the bowels of Hell.

Geronimo reached down through the steam and the stench, grabbed Red Eye's cane and ran for shore. The moment he set foot on East Bay Street, the wharf moaned and rattled like chains and collapsed. All six men who witnessed the fight were swept away … six grown men and one teenager from Wadmalaw Island.

The storm cleared and Leon Jr., his boats and crews arrived at the spot where Gadsden's Wharf used to be. The search for survivors commenced. The fleet had not left the landing that day because of the storm. By midnight all the bodies except one had been recovered. Jacob's was not among them.

For months Leon Jr. searched for his nephew until the coroner finally declared the boy was lost at sea. There was no funeral for Jacob Rouse in Charleston. But a memorial service for him on Wadmalaw was well attended by family and friends, including Geronimo Watson, who was still on the lam. Cousin Emma was not among them. She never believed Jacob died that stormy day in the fall of 1917. And she wasn't the only one.

# EPILOGUE

Twenty-one years have passed since Jacob disappeared in the roiling waters of Charleston harbor. During that time his grandmother died peacefully in her eighty-second year as she sat in her rocking chair, holding her pipe, on the porch of her little house on Wadmalaw Island. Hazel, her loving daughter-in-law, was there when Mary passed. Hazel said Mary never shed a tear over Jacob's disappearance, telling anyone who listened that *"de ol' folk"* believe it is not possible for a person born with the veil and the mark of the cross to drown.

Before she passed away, Mary had said Jacob visited her from time to time, especially on winter nights as she sat alone in her living room by the fire, smoked her pipe and analyzed the flames. When folks heard her talking like this, they nodded, smiled graciously and quickly changed the subject. After all, Mary was up in years.

But Cousin Emma, Leon Jr. and Hazel were not among the doubters. Hazel had often gone to Wadmalaw Island by boat to visit Mary, and they were extremely close by the time she died. Hazel credited both Mary and Jacob with helping conquer her fear of drowning. She often thought about that boat turning over in the Waccamaw River and her loved ones perishing in the depths. She never forgot the stranger near the shore who pulled her to safety. Hazel became wise and a beloved spiritual community leader in Charleston.

About a year after Jacob went missing, Leon Jr. and Hazel had their first child, a son they named Leon II. Two years later their daughter, April, arrived. Hazel made sure her children received spiritual names in ceremonies on Wadmalaw, much to Mary's delight. Leon II was fourteen years old and April was twelve when their great-grandmother passed. Leon Jr. took his family to the island for Memorial Day festivities every year. When a bridge was built to Wadmalaw, he drove his family to the island from their house in uptown Charleston.

Each Saturday of Memorial Day weekends, Leon Jr., Hazel and the children spent hours cleaning up around their ancestors' graves. Afterward, Leon would gather his family under the gnarly limbs of the cemetery's lone live oak and talk about their Gullah kinfolk and traditions. Mary was laid to rest in that cemetery between the graves of her husband, Big Leon, and her daughter Anna.

One year, Leon Jr. and his family gathered around Mary's grave and he said:

"Today I go' tell yah 'bout Cu'zin Jacob, whose spirrut name is Moya Samba. I'm convinced that Jacob, who was born with the veil and had an unusual birthmark that looked like a cross on his shoulder, had been in dis worl' long befo' he came hey. I beleeb' 'e ent nebuh die, dat Jacob wuh sent by Gawd to Jalapa Island on a mission."

The children listened spellbound, one might say, to what their father was saying:

"… I beleeb' Jacob wuh an emissary ob de Lawd, sent to help folk lib'n round hey since slabery time — and dat a long time ago. Dey wuh po' in de pocketbook buh not in de spirrut, and dey 'preciate all Jacob do fuh 'em."

Leon Jr. was convinced *Moya Samba* first arrived at the behest of the great African spirit called *Nkisi* to live on Jalapa Island. He said he learned that Jalapa is a "*mwelo*," which means "a door between two worlds." He also said that whenever *Moya Samba* had a mission, he would be reborn in human form under the veil and bearing the special birthmark. Big Leon, who was one of God's special emissaries, served as Jacob's guide.

"Moya Samba fust came to the S.C. Lowcountry with de fust Africans all dem year ago, an' he been comin' back round ebuh since to bring peace, harmony and love to de Gullah people."

That's when Leon II asked his father, *"Did Jacob… I mean… Moya Samba come see Nana after he fell off the wharf?"*

"Uh-huh," Leon Jr. said. *'Das wuh Nana told me not long befo' she pass.*

On the coldest winter nights she would fall asleep in her chair in front ob de fire. Nana say, she would hea' de front door creak open, and in step Jacob — smilin' like he always do, wid 'e arm full ob chop wood. 'Jacob, dat you?' she axed. 'Yes ma'am,' Jacob say, and he look like Big Leon standin' dey.' Dat wuh Nana tell me."

Leon told the children he was convinced that Jacob could communicate with those who went before him, and that the spirit of Big Leon taught him about roots and herbs growing wild on Jalapa Island and elsewhere in the South Carolina Lowcountry. Leon Jr. said Jacob told his grandmother the spiritual world was far different than this one. He said *Moya Samba* moved from one realm to the other and back again.

That's what Leon Jr. told his children that day in the cemetery, adding:

"Nana say all dem star yah see at night are spirrut goin' back and forth to Jalapa an' oduh place like dat. Dey 'Standin' en de Gap' fuh folk dat need 'em, an' Jacob one ob 'em. Dat wuh Nana told me."

THE END

ABOUT THE AUTHOR

SHERMAN E. PYATT is a native of Charleston, South Carolina. He received his B.A. degree from Johnson C. Smith University and his MLIS from Indiana University. He later received certification in archival sciences from Georgia State University. Pyatt has served as research librarian, interim director, and archivist at The Citadel Military College, The Avery Research Center at the College of Charleston and at South Carolina State University. His publications include *Martin Luther King, Jr., An Annotated Bibliography* (Greenwood Press, 1986). *Apartheid: A Selective Annotated Bibliography*, 1978-1987 (Garland Publishing, 1990). *A Dictionary and Catalog of African American Folklife of the South* (Greenwood Press, 1999). *Charleston South Carolina: Black America Series* (Arcadia Publishing, 2000). *Burke High School: 1894-2006* (Arcadia Publishing, 2007). *The Other Side of Skillet: Healthy and Alternative Eating in the Lowcountry* (Lulu Publishing, 2015). He serves as a volunteer with several Lowcountry organizations and served as a commissioner on the Gullah Geechee Cultural Heritage Corridor (2016-2020). Pyatt currently serves as a volunteer at the International African American Museum in Charleston.

GULLAH GLOSSARY

—A—

ABOA'D	aboard
AFREEKA	Africa
AFTUH	after
ALIBE	alive
ANUDDUH	another
AX	ask
AXE	tool to chop wood
AX'UM	ask him, her

—B—

'BACCA	tobacco
BAD MOUT'	bad mouth; a spell, a form of curse
BATT'RY	Battery
BES'	best
BETTUH	better
BEWFU'T	Beaufort, S.C.
B'FO'	before
BIGGUH	bigger
BIN	been, was
B'LEEB	believe
BOA'D	board, boards
BODDUH	bother
BOFF	both
BO'N	born
BOOTIFUL	beautiful
'BOUT	about
BREAT'	breath
BREKWUS	breakfast, breakfasts
BRUDDUH	brother
BUCKRA	white man (sometimes derogatory)

BUDDUH	butter
BUH	but
BUZZUT	buzzard, buzzards

— C —

'CEPT	except
CHASS'TUN	Charleston, S.C.
CHIL'	child
CHILLUM	children
CHRIS'MUS	Christmas
CHU'CH	church
CHUNK	throw
COL'	cold
COLLUH	color, colors
COPPUH	copper
CRACK 'E TEET	opened her or his mouth to speak
CRIK	creek, creeks
CROKUHSACK	croaker, croker, burlap
CULLUD	colored, black, brown, mixed race
CUZ'N	cousin
CYAS'NET	cast net for taking shrimp & mullet

— D —

DAS DE TRUTE	that's the truth
DAS	that's
DAT	that
DAUGHTUH	daughter, daughters
DAYCLEAN	broad daylight just after sun-up
DE	the
DEM	them, those
DERE	there
DEY	they, there
DINNUH	dinner
DIS	this, just
DO'N	doing
DON'	don't, doesn't

DUH   is, do, does

— E —

'E	he, she, it
EBBUH	ever
EBBUHLASTIN'	everlasting
EB'N	even
EB'RY	every
EBERYBODY	everybody
EBERYT'ING	everything
EEBEN	even
EEBNIN'	evening
EEDUH	either
ELEBEN	eleven
'EM	them
ENT	ain't
ENTY	ain't it, isn't it

— F —

FABUH	favor
FAC'	fact
FAIT	faith
FAMBLY	family
FAS'	fast
FAUDUH	father
FEWTUH	future
FIAH	fire
FLOUNDA'	flounder
FO'	four
FO'TEEN	fourteen
FRUM	from
FUH	for
FUH'EBUH	forever
FUHGIBNESS	forgiveness
FUHGIT	forget
FUH TRUE	in truth, the truth

FULL 'EM	fill them
FUSH	fish
FUST	first

— G —

GAL	girl, girls
GAWD	God, God's
GIB'	give, gives, gave
GIF'	gift
GIMME	give me, gave me
GIT	get, gets, got
GO	going
GRABE	grave, graves
GRAN'	gran'
GRATE	great
GRIT	grits
GWINE	going

— H —

HAB	have, has, had
HABIN'	having
HAFUH	has, have to
HAG	a house witch
HAPP'N	happen
HEA'	hear
HEABEN	Heaven
HEABY	heavy
HE'P	help
HEY	here, hear
HOL'	hold
HONGRY	hungry
HUCCOME	how come
HUH	how
HUNNUH	how are you
HUH YUH DUH?	How are you doing?

— I —

INIT   Isn't

— J —

JEDUS   Jesus
JIS   just
JISSO   just so
JOGRAPHY   geography

— K —

KETCH'UM   catch him, her
KIN   can
KIND'UH   kind of
KIN'T   can't
KNO'   know

— L —

LAS'   last, lasts
LAWD   Lord
LEEBE   leave
LEF'   left
LEMME   let me
LIB   live
LIL'   little
LONGUH   longer
LOT'UH   a lot of
LUB   love
LUMBUH-Y'AD   lumberyard

— M —

MA'AM   madam
MANNUS   manners
MARRI'D   married
MEKE   make
'MEMBUH   remember

MO'	more
MOMMA	mother
MONT'	month, months
MOOB	move
MORN'N	morning
MOUT'	mouth
MUH	my
MUSSY	mercy

—N—

NEBUH	never
'NUF	enough
NUM'	numb
NUTT'N	nothing

—O—

OB	of
OBUH	over
OBUHBOA'D	overboard
ODDUH	other
OFF'UN	often
OFFUH	offer
OL'	old
'OOMAN	woman

—P—

PEOLA	light-color skin
PERLO	pilaf, rice steamed with seafood/meat
PO'CH	porch
PREACHUH	preacher
PURTY	pretty

—R—

'RAP UP	Wrapped up

— S —

SABE	save
'SCUSE	excuse
SETT'N'UP	sitting up night before funeral
SHA'AK	shark
SHO'	sure
SHO'E	shore
SISTUH	sister
SKAY'D	scared
SKRAIT	straight
SKREET	street
SKRENGT'	strength
SMUDDUH	smother, smothered
'SPENSIVE	expensive
SPIRRUT	spirit
SPOSE	suppose
ST'AT, STATIN'	start, starting
STOBE	stove
STO'M	storm
SUMP'N	something
'SUMPTION	consumption; pneumonia
SUPPUH	supper
SWAYTOGAWD	swear to God
SWEETMOUT'	flatter
SWIMP(S)	shrimp

— T —

T'ANK	thank
T'ANKFUL	thankful
T'ANK YAH	thank you
TAS'E	taste
T'DAY	today
TEET'	teeth
TEK	take
TENSHUN	attention
T'GETHUH	together

THU'STY	thirsty
TIEF	thief, steal
TING	thing
TINK	think
T'MORRUH	tomorrow
TOTE	carry
TRABEL	travel
T'REE	three
T'ROW	throw

— U —

'UM	him, her, them, it
UNDUH	under
UNDUHSTAN'	understand

— W —

WAN'	want
WAN'UH	want to
WEDD'N	wedding
WEDDUH	weather
WEY	where
WEY'EBUH	where ever
WID	with
WINDUH	windows
WONDRIN	wondering
WOPP'UH	whopper, tall tale
WUFFUH	what for, why
WUH	what, was
WUNDUH	wonder

— X —

'XACTLY	exactly

— Y —

YA'D	yard
YAH	you

YEAH year
YISTIDDY yesterday
YUH here

www.ingramcontent.com/pod-product-compliance
Lightning Source LLC
Chambersburg PA
CBHW032122020726
47494CB00007BA/2193